The Little House
Family Tree

_m._   Lewis Tucker

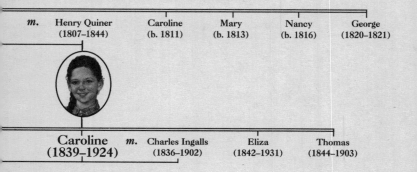

_m._   Henry Quiner   Caroline   Mary   Nancy   George
(1807–1844)   (b. 1811)   (b. 1813)   (b. 1816)   (1820–1821)

Caroline   _m._   Charles Ingalls   Eliza   Thomas
(1839–1924)   (1836–1902)   (1842–1931)   (1844–1903)

Caroline   Charles   Grace
(1870–1946)   (1875–1876)   (1877–1941)

Murphy   Q

Little House
in the Highlands

Melissa Wiley

Illustrations by Renée Graef

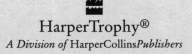

HarperTrophy®
A Division of HarperCollinsPublishers

*For Scott, who makes the
hills and valleys roar*

*Special thanks to Caroline Carr-Locke for digging up
detailed information about customs and cultures in late-eighteenth-
century Scotland and much gratitude to Norman Kennedy for his
wonderful recordings of Scottish folk music.*

Harper Trophy®, ☕®, Little House®, and The Martha Years™
are trademarks of HarperCollins Publishers Inc.

Little House in the Highlands
Text copyright © 1999 by HarperCollins Publishers Inc.
Illustrations © 1999 by Renée Graef
Printed in the United States of America. For information address
HarperCollins Children's Books, a division of HarperCollins Publishers,
10 East 53rd Street, New York, NY 10022.
http://www.harperchildrens.com

Library of Congress Cataloging-in-Publication Data
Wiley, Melissa.
    Little house in the Highlands / Melissa Wiley ; illustrations by
Renée Graef.
        p.   cm. — (The Martha years)
    Summary: The childhood adventures in the Scottish countryside of
six-year-old Martha Morse, who would grow up to become the great-
grandmother of author Laura Ingalls Wilder.
    ISBN 0-06-027983-4. — ISBN 0-06-028202-9 (lib. bdg.)
    ISBN 0-06-440712-8 (pbk.)
    [1. Family life—Scotland—Fiction.   2. Scotland—Fiction.]   I. Graef,
Renée, ill.   II. Title.   III. Series: Wiley, Melissa.   Martha years.
PZ7.W64814Li   1999   98-34910
[Fic]—dc21   CIP
                                                                  AC

9   10

❖

First Edition, 1999

Contents

The Friendly Valley

Loch Caraid was a small blue lake tucked into a Scottish mountain valley. On its shore were a half dozen cottages that had no names and one stately house that did. It was called the Stone House, and a little girl named Martha Morse lived there with her family many, many years ago.

The name of the valley was Glencaraid. That meant "Friendly Valley," and Loch Caraid meant "Friendly Lake." The people who lived in the valley had a story about those names. One summer evening, when it was just cool enough for a fire made of peat grass to flicker on the hearth, Martha heard the story from her mother.

Martha's three brothers and her one sister were downstairs in the kitchen begging plums from the cook. Her father was busy at his writing table. Father was laird of the estate of Glencaraid, and he had important letters to write. So just for now, Martha had Mum all to herself in the cozy corner beside the hearth of Mum and Father's big bedroom. The scratching of Father's feather pen was a pleasant accompaniment to Mum's story and the soft whirring of her spinning wheel.

"It was many hundreds of years ago," Mum was saying, "that a man named Edward MacNab caught his first glimpse of the loch from high above on the mountainside."

"MacNab!" Martha said. "But we're MacNabs!"

"Aye." Mum nodded. "That we are. You have MacNab blood on both sides, for your father's grandfather married a MacNab girl, and my own mother was of that clan. Although your name be Morse, my lass, you're more MacNab than aught else."

"Is your mother in the story?" Martha wanted to know.

Mum laughed. "Och, nay! This happened long years before my mother was even dreamed of, or her mother, or *her* mother. Now—shall I go on?"

"Aye!" Martha nodded, her long red curls bouncing on her shoulders. She scooted her stool closer to Mum so that she could hear better above the spinning wheel's hum. Beneath Mum's fingers golden-brown flax fibers twisted into one long, spider-thin thread. The peat fire glowed and crackled. Even though it was summer, the mountain wind carried a chill to the valley at night.

Mum's tale spun out above the thread. Edward MacNab, she told Martha, had been traveling for a very long time. He was bone-tired and hoped to see the smoke of a chimney in the valley below, for he had a longing to spend the night in a warm bed.

But the evening was misty and dim. All

Edward could see of the valley was the dark water of the lake at the foot of the mountains. In the gloomy light it looked exactly like a mouth waiting to swallow anyone who dared climb down. Not far from the lake were two little ponds that looked just like two angry, staring eyes. Edward MacNab shuddered and gave a low whistle.

"'Tis no a friendly sort of a place, that!" he said. He spoke aloud, for he thought there was no one around to hear. But he was wrong. He was not alone.

A water fairy lived in the lake, and she had wandered onto the mountain that evening to gather mist from the rocky crags. When she saw Edward, she wrapped some shreds of mist around her so she wouldn't be seen. And she would have stayed hidden, if only he had spoken more wisely—or not at all.

"But it is ever the gift and the curse of a MacNab to speak the thoughts that pop into his mind," Mum told Martha. "Your father has it, and so do you, my bold wee lass. As soon as you could speak, you were saying things

4

aloud that others would only dare to think. Never will I forget the first time you met auld Laird Alroch. Marched right up to him, you did, and asked if it was true he was bald as an egg under his wig!"

"But what about the water fairy?" Martha said impatiently. She had already heard the story of what she had once said to the kind old gentleman who lived on the other side of the mountains. Fairies were much more interesting.

"Well," Mum went on, "it did not sit well with the fairy to hear this stranger speaking of her loch in that way. She crept up to Edward and laid one pale hand on his shoulder. Quick as a wink she turned him to stone.

"'Not friendly, is it?' she said to Edward— for though his body was frozen in rock, he had yet the senses of a man and could hear her. Edward stared at the water fairy with his stone eyes that could not blink.

"Her skin was whiter than new-bleached linen. Her hair was the pale green of a spring leaf just opening on the twig, and it fell in ripples all the way to her feet. She had slanting green eyes and a little pointed chin. Edward MacNab thought he had never seen aught so lovely."

Martha thought to herself that the fairy must have looked like Mum, except Mum's eyes were blue and her hair was a rich golden brown instead of pale green. She wore it piled high on her head in a mass of shining waves. Her blue eyes always had a laugh peeking out of them, even now when her brows were drawn together fiercely in imitation of the water fairy's anger.

Mum's lilting voice grew cold and furious as she spoke the fairy's words. "'Who are you to judge this loch?' the water fairy said. 'You who set eyes on it for the first time not five minutes ago? I'll not have you speaking ill of my home!' Her eyes blazed like two coals burning through a white sheet. Inside his stone skin Edward MacNab quaked. He wondered if he would spend the rest of his days as a boulder on this mountain."

"Did he, Mum?" Martha asked, then shook

her head thoughtfully. "Nay, he couldna have. I've never seen any boulder up there that looks like a man."

Mum laughed. Martha was the youngest of the five Morse children, but Mum said she was sharper than a new pin. Father said it was a pity she wasn't a boy, for she'd have made a fine lawyer with her way of seeing the holes in a tale.

"Do you have the telling of this story, or do I?" Mum said. "And here I was thinking you wanted to hear the end of it."

"I do, I do!" Martha cried. "I'll be quiet."

"Aye, when pigs fly," Mum teased. "Well, Edward had luck on his side. This water fairy was kinder-hearted than many of her race. She told him he would be under the spell for just a year and a day. 'You shall stand here sunup and sundown,' said she, 'and watch this loch in all its moods. We will see then if you can say it is not a friendly sort of place.'"

"A year and a day! But that's a terrible long time!" Martha burst out, and then clapped a hand over her mouth. She had promised to be quiet.

"Aye," said Mum, winking at her, "but not so long as forever." She stopped to wrap a new bundle of flax onto the distaff of her spinning wheel. Martha squirmed on her stool. It was hard to wait. At last Mum was back in her chair, her foot tapping on the treadle and the wheel whirring its soft hum.

Then Mum told how Edward MacNab had had to sit frozen on the mountain through all the long days and weeks of a year. He could not eat or sleep or stretch his legs. He could only watch, and listen, and wait. Martha thought about how hard it was to sit still for half the morning in church. She would not have liked to be in Edward MacNab's shoes.

The worst of it was, not a single day had passed before Edward knew that the water fairy was right. When the sun rose the next morning, he saw before him a lake bluer than the sky. Little wind-ripples danced across it. Golden light glinted off the lake and the two small ponds nearby. A rich valley opened out around the water and climbed gently to the hills. The heather on the hillsides was a purple the like of which Edward had never seen before. Even the gray and craggy mountains were no longer forbidding, but seemed instead like gentle guards keeping watch over the lovely loch and its valley.

"Long and long were the nights Edward had to wait through," Mum said. "But the days were a joy to him, for no one could ever get tired of looking at our lake."

At last the year and the day had passed. The fairy returned and laid a hand on Edward's stone shoulder. Instantly he was flesh once more.

"'Tis right you were, miss, and I beg your pardon," he said. "A friendlier spot I never saw. In fact, I'm of a mind to end my travels right here—if it be all right with you. Many leagues have I come seekin' a place to build a home. I canna think of a better spot than right there on the shores of that loch."

The fairy was pleased, and she said that he

might stay. So Edward built a house in the valley, and in time he found a wife to live in it with him. And he told his children the story of the water fairy, and they told their children and grandchildren. And so it went for hundreds of years, until all the people around knew the lake as Loch Caraid, the Friendly Lake, and the valley as Glencaraid, the Friendly Valley.

"But Mum," said Martha, when her mother had finished the tale, "what happened to the two little ponds that looked like eyes? There aren't any ponds in the glen."

"Och," said Mum, "there's a tail to the story. The fairy didna want anyone else thinking those ponds looked like staring round eyes, spoiling the pretty view of the valley. And besides, she'd been thinking she'd like a bit more room in her own nice loch. So she rolled up the two little ponds into a linen sheet and shook them out into Loch Caraid!"

Martha couldn't see how you would go about rolling a pond up in a linen sheet without all the water soaking through, but everyone knew that fairies had special tricks of their own. They could live for hundreds of years, and so they had time to learn lots of things that mortals didn't know.

"I've never seen any fairy in the loch," she said. "Is she still there?"

"Keep your eyes open and your wits about you," said Mum, "and who knows what you might see someday? The Good People are wary. You'll not see them unless they want you to."

Martha made up her mind that she would see that fairy someday, sure as water was wet. As soon as she was old enough to go out in the rowboat with her brother Duncan, who was her best playmate, she would go looking for the beautiful green-haired lady.

But she was only six and a half, and Duncan had just turned eight. Father said they could not go out in the boat alone until they were much older. Half seven seemed plenty old enough to Martha, but Father was firm. And what Father said went, for he was Laird Glencaraid.

Everyone in the valley was under Father's care. He owned all the land north to the tip of the valley and south almost to the village of Clachan. That land had been in his family for hundreds of years—ever since Edward MacNab built his house there, in fact.

Father had inherited Glencaraid from his MacNab grandmother years ago, before Martha was born. Her older sister, Grisie, had been just a wee girl when the title passed to Father. Her brother Alisdair had been the tiniest of babies. Now Grisie was a great girl of fourteen, nearly grown up, and Alisdair was twelve.

Robbie, who was eleven now, had been born the year Father began to build the new house. Duncan was the first baby born in the Stone House, in Mum and Father's big bedroom above the parlor. Martha was born there too. She liked to climb into her parents' big bed with the green plaid curtains that hung round it, and try to remember being a tiny baby in Mum's arms. Try as she might, she could not remember it.

But now it was nearly time to go to her own

bed in the nursery. Grisie and the boys came clattering up the stairs, munching the last of their plums. Robbie had a half-eaten plum in each hand. As he came into the room, a third plum slipped out from under his arm and rolled across the floor.

"Oops!" he said to Martha through a juicy mouthful. "That one was yours."

Martha wrinkled her nose at him, and he made a face back at her, wiping plum juice off his chin with his sleeve.

"Robert!" Mum scolded. "We've napkins for that."

Martha fished her plum out from under a chair. It was bruised, but just a little.

"Here, Martha," Duncan said, offering her a new plum. "You can have mine."

"Nay, this one's all right," she said. She smiled at Duncan. He always stuck up for her when Robbie teased. Everyone said Duncan and Robbie looked so much alike they could be twins, except for the three years' difference in their ages. But although they had the same thick brown hair curling on their necks and the same dark-lashed blue eyes, they were really nothing alike. Robbie was bold and loud, and he had something to say about everything. Duncan liked to keep his thoughts to himself around most people. When he was alone with Martha, then he would talk and talk, telling her stories about the daring adventures they would have together someday. He had a calm, steady gaze that Cook said was wise as an owl's and twice as uncanny.

Martha bit into her plum. It was tangy-sweet and delicious. Duncan and Robbie were taking turns tossing their plum pits into the fire. When Martha had finished eating, she threw hers in too. Alisdair and Grisie were too old for playing games with plum pits. Grisie sat quietly on her stool, her dark hair shining in the firelight. She sat with her back very straight, taking small, careful bites. Robbie could eat five plums in the time it took Grisie to eat one.

Alisdair ate slowly too, but it was not because he was neat. He was in fact always a little rumpled, with his waistcoat buttoned wrong or his red hair falling into his eyes. He had a long, thin face and long, thin hands. In one of them he held a plum with one big bite taken out of it, but he had picked up Father's copy of *Scots Magazine* and was leafing through it, forgetting to eat. The magazine came by post all the way from Edinburgh several times a year. Sometimes there were stories in it, and Mum or Alisdair would read them aloud to the rest of the family.

When at last Alisdair had finished eating, he gave the pit to Martha. She tossed it into the fire and watched it raise a shower of sparks from the peat. Then Mum said it was getting late, and she rose from her spinning.

"Get into your nightclothes and I'll be right along to tuck you in," she told Martha. She said the same thing every night. It gave Martha a nice comfortable feeling to hear those words. Even if she was very sleepy, she would wait on her stool until Mum said them.

Martha picked up her doll, Lady Flora, from the cradle beside Mum's bed. Martha had slept in that cradle when she was a tiny baby, and so had Duncan, and Robbie, and Alisdair, and Grisie—only Father liked to joke that Robbie had never slept at all. Robbie was still the last one to go to sleep and the first one to wake up in the morning. But now he slept in a big bed in the nursery with Duncan. All the children slept in the nursery, but Father said Grisie and Alisdair were getting so big, he'd soon need to think about adding another room to the house.

Martha crept to Father's side to say good-night. The light of an oil lamp on the writing table spilled over his close-cropped red hair and made a shadow beneath his strong, square jaw. His white wig with the tightly rolled curls rested on its stand beside the table. Father looked up from his letter and smiled at Martha.

"Have you had your fill of stories for one night, then?" he asked.

"Oh, no, Father. I still want to know where Edward MacNab found his wife, and what the water fairy does with the mist she gets from the mountain."

Father shook his head in mock dismay. "Och, Martha Gráinne Morse, the Judgment Day could be upon us and you'd stand there spouting questions about what happens to the sheep when the farmers go to heaven!"

"But what *will* happen to them, Father? I'd like to know."

"Aye, and I'd like to know how many days my men have to cut the peats before it rains. You'll never find as many answers as you have questions, Martha."

He gave her a kiss. Martha held up Lady Flora for her own kiss, and Father solemnly brushed his lips against the wooden cheek. Then he turned back to his letter.

Martha went across the hall to the nursery. She snuggled in next to Grisie, ready to dream about stone men and green-haired ladies, and sailing with Duncan on a glittering, friendly lake.

The Stone House

The first sound Martha heard each
morning was the bang of a box-bed
door sliding open. All the beds in the
nursery had wooden walls built around them
and wooden ceilings on top, so that each bed
was like its own tiny room. Alisdair had a
box bed all to himself, Robbie shared with
Duncan, and there was a third bed for Martha
and Grisie.

At night, after Mum tucked Martha in and
gave her a kiss, she gently slid the bed's door-
panel closed. It was very dark inside, but it

was warm and cozy, and Martha could snuggle up next to Grisie and listen to the sound of her brothers' breathing from their beds across the room.

The loud bang that started every morning was Robbie, in a hurry to get out of bed. Duncan would grumble sleepily and slide the panel closed again, to block out the sunlight streaming in through the nursery windows. But Robbie always made a lot of noise getting dressed, so that before he was finished everyone else was awake. Father said that Robbie was better than a rooster.

After the door-banging and the slapping of Robbie's feet on the floor came the soft sound of the housemaid's humming. Martha always waited in bed until she heard Mollie enter the nursery, bringing the music of the hills with her. Martha loved to listen to the old Gaelic work songs and ballads that hung in the air around Mollie like birds. Like her brothers and sister, Martha could speak Gaelic as well as English, and she thought songs sounded prettier in the ancient language of the Highlands.

"Fuirich an diu gus am maireach . . ." lilted Mollie's soft voice this morning, "Wait today until tomorrow." But Martha couldn't wait any longer. The smell of warm porridge had filled the air along with Mollie's song. Martha slid open the door-panel and climbed out of bed.

Grisie sat up sleepily behind her, rubbing her eyes. "I might as well be sharing the bed with a cow, Martha. What makes you kick so in your sleep?"

"You wouldna feel it if you'd keep to your own side," Martha retorted. Grisie was always grumpy in the mornings.

Martha hurried to the hearth, where Mollie had hung the black pot of oatmeal porridge from a hook over the fire. Mollie smiled a good morning at Martha without dropping a note of her song nor stopping her work. She always said she never could get her hands to work if she wasn't singing. Her voice was clear and sweet, like a lark's. But Martha thought Mollie was more like a little brown field mouse, with her sandy hair, her sharp, freckled face, and her brisk movements. She wore a striped skirt and a plaid apron, tied in back with a stiff bow that quivered up and down as she moved.

It quivered now as she laid out two pots of cream and five pewter spoons upon the hearth-stones. The cream looked fresh and thick. It had been cooling on the marble shelf in the dairy since yesterday's milking. Martha's stomach rumbled.

The good porridge smell chased the last sleepiness out of the room. Robbie stuck his finger in the cream-pot, and Grisie stalked to the fireside to scold him. Robbie made a face at her. Ever since their governess had gotten married and moved away two springs ago, Grisie acted like she was in charge of the nursery. She would be fifteen in the fall, and Mum said she could put her hair up then. Right now Grisie's thick dark hair streamed halfway down her back. Martha liked to watch it sway from side to side when Grisie walked. She would be sorry when Grisie began to wear it twisted up off her neck.

Alisdair and Duncan crawled out of their beds and crowded around the hearth with the others. Breakfast in the nursery was a standing-up meal. Still humming her Gaelic tune, Mollie filled two big bowls with the hot porridge and set one next to each cream-pot on the hearth-stones. Then she gave the fire one last poke and hurried to the doorway. Mornings were Mollie's busy time.

"Mind ye eat a bit o' porridge with yer cream, Miss Martha," she called back over her shoulder on her way down the hall to Father and Mum's bedroom.

Martha stopped with her spoon halfway to the cream-pot. Cool, rich cream was the best-tasting thing in the world. But it was good mixed with the warm porridge, too. She took a spoonful of porridge from the bowl and dipped it into the cream-pot. The thick white liquid pooled over the sweet oats. Cook always stirred a little brown sugar into the children's breakfast porridge. Alisdair and Grisie shared one bowl of porridge and one pot of cream, and Martha shared with Duncan. Robbie stood in the middle, dipping his spoon into both bowls. Martha thought he got more that way, but it was hard to tell. It didn't matter anyway. By the time the big bowl of porridge was empty, and every drop of cream was gone, Martha was very full.

Alisdair and Duncan went behind the tall wooden screen in the corner of the nursery to get dressed. Robbie went off to Father and Mum's room to see if there was any porridge left from their breakfast. While the girls waited for their turn behind the screen, Grisie sat down on the hearth to brush Martha's hair. Martha had a little stool to sit on while Grisie worked through the tangles. She liked this part of the morning. Sometimes Grisie fussed a little while she brushed. But her hands were always gentle and she never pulled Martha's hair.

"The fairies must have been here last night," Grisie told Martha. "They've tangled your hair into a dozen elf-locks! If you'd keep your nightcap on they couldna get at your hair, you know."

"I dinna take it off on purpose," Martha said. "It comes off when I'm asleep." Her toes

found a hole in the floorboard beneath her. A lot of the floorboards had holes bored in them, from when the boards were roped together for their journey north from the lumberyards of Lochearnhead. It was the job of Sandy, Father's steward, to keep the holes plugged up. But the plugs were always falling out and landing with a plop in the room beneath. Martha held her nightgown out of the way and peered through the hole to the kitchen below. She thought she could see Cook's hand, stirring something in a white bowl.

"Hold your head up straight!" Grisie said. "'Tis nearly finished I am, if you'll just sit still."

After Grisie was done with Martha's hair, it was time to get dressed. The boys had gone downstairs. Grisie helped Martha into her blue plaid petticoat and dress and tied her dust-gown in the back. The dust-gown was like a long cotton apron with sleeves. Martha didn't like to wear it, but Mum said she must. It kept her dresses from getting too dirty.

Grisie did not have to wear a dust-gown.

She never got a spot on her dresses, not even the white ones. She tied a sash below the bodice of her yellow linen gown, which had once been a dress of Mum's. Last spring it had been cut down to fit Grisie. Martha remembered that Mum would be getting dressed now. She ran to Mum's room.

Mum was just stepping into her petticoat. Mollie helped her tie the laces. Since Mum was not expecting visitors today, she put on only a plain linen everyday dress. It was a soft gray color, with long, tight sleeves and a high waist. The slim bodice was trimmed with a little froth of lace. Mollie pinned up the back and straightened out Mum's long, full skirt. Martha thought Mum looked like a queen, even with her plain dress and her hair hidden by the flowered lawn cap she wore in the mornings.

The bedroom was sunny and bright. Outside the east windows morning light shimmered on the lake. The tall top section of each window had real glass in it. The bottom section had no glass, only wooden shutters that could be thrown wide to let in the breeze and the scent of heather. The kitchen had the same kind of windows. But in the parlor the windows had panes of glass all the way down. They were very beautiful, with the crisp dark lines of wood dividing the panes. But they could not be easily opened. Martha was glad there were shutters in the bedrooms and the kitchen. She loved the fresh smell of heather.

Mum had finished dressing now and said she must look over the food stores, for it was nearly time to send Sandy, the steward, to town to buy sugar and spices. Martha went down the stone staircase to the kitchen, to see if Cook was baking pies today.

The Stone House was the only house in the valley with an upstairs and a downstairs. It had stone walls and a gray slate roof and smooth wooden floors. There were two chimneys, one on each end of the roof. Upstairs were the nursery and the bedroom, and downstairs were the big kitchen and the parlor.

Martha could not imagine a grander house than hers, with two whole stories and an attic. It had a kitchen that was a room all by itself, and a parlor for company, and real glass window-panes. But Alisdair said it was really quite a little house, compared to the houses some lairds lived in. He had been over the mountain to Laird Alroch's castle, so he knew. Laird Alroch had fifteen rooms and a front hall made of marble. And the Duke of Atholl at Blair Castle in the north had so many rooms that he used three as dining rooms and three as drawing rooms, and another whole room for a library!

Martha wandered into the kitchen. Today was not a pie day, after all. There was no piecrust on Cook's table, nor any sweet baking smell in the air. There was only the rich brown smell of the broth that was always simmering in the big iron cauldron that hung in one end of the fireplace. There was hardly a day in the year that Cook did not serve a hearty broth with dinner.

The huge fireplace ran along the west wall of the kitchen. It was so big, Martha could have stood inside it and stretched her arms out with room to spare, if the fire had ever been put out. There were three long benches set into the earthen floor around the hearth, where the servants sat to eat their dinners. Against one kitchen wall were barrels of barley flour and oats and sugar. Another wall was lined with tall stacks of peats for the fire. The peat grass had been cut from the ground in great matted squares that burned as well as wood, only faster. Now the squares were piled against the wall nearly to the roof beams.

Tucked into the back corner of the kitchen, next to the staircase wall, were Cook's bed and washbasin. Mollie shared a bed with Nannie, the kitchenmaid, up in the attic among rolls of handspun yarn and chests of linen. Sandy lived in one of the cottages on the lakeshore with his wife and his seven children. He came to the Stone House early every morning to do chores around the house and garden, and to answer the door when visitors came.

"Good mornin' to ye, Miss Martha!" Cook smiled at her from one of the benches by the hearth, where she sat shelling peas. Her broad hands moved quickly above the bowl in her lap, shaking peas out of their pods and casting the pods into a bucket on the floor. She was a large woman with a round red face and a stubborn chin. Her gray hair was hidden beneath a tight white cap that made her red face look even redder.

Martha climbed up beside Cook and sat for a while, swinging her feet back and forth, back and forth, and every now and then sneaking a pea from Cook's bowl.

"The broth wants stirrin'," Cook said. "Happen ye'd like to do it?"

"Aye!" Martha cried. It felt very grown-up to stand before the fire and stir the soup in the big black cauldron. Bits of onion and a bundle of sweet herbs bobbed to the surface from time to time, like little fish showing their heads in a pond. Sometimes the spoon bumped into the big chunk of beef in the bottom of the pot.

Martha loved to sit in the kitchen with Cook and listen to her stories. Cook had worked in a castle before she came to Glencaraid, long ago when she was a young girl. It had been nearly as big as Blair Castle. Cook said she would not work in a great house like that again for all the world. There had been one hundred and seventeen stairs, and they all had to be scrubbed once a week. The silver service was so large that it took three girls two whole afternoons to polish it.

"Rub until me arms seemed like to fall off, I would, and still there'd be heaps of silver left to get through!" she told Martha. "If ye thought too hard of all the work piled up, ye'd want to just sit doon and weep. And hungry all the time, I was, for nivver was there enough for the servants to eat. The worst of it was, we all had our meals in the dining hall at one great long table. The laird's family sat up at the head and the servants sat at the foot. Heaps of fine food we'd bring out from the kitchen, and all of it went at the head of the table in front of the laird. Roast beef, fresh butter, bowls of plums and apricots, and always a big platter of oysters from the sea loch. Och, the sight o' it all! Along about the middle o' the table came a couple of tough old hens for the governess, the chaplain, and such—them as worked in the house but was far above the likes of us kitchenmaids. Down at the foot where my place was, all we had was barley cakes and a weak broth. Bitter hard it was, to gnaw on an old stale cake with the smell of roast beef floating down from the head of the table!"

Cook shuddered, remembering. A pea popped loose from its pod and rolled across the floor. Martha ran after it. "Ye mind me words, Miss Martha," Cook said. "'Tis better to live in a little house where there's no more work than can be done in a day, and decent food for everyone, than in the finest castle in the county where every soul has either too much or too little than is good for them!"

Martha hoped she would see a fine castle someday. But she would not like to live in one, if it was as Cook said.

"I'd have made them give you some beef," she told Cook hotly. She could not understand how the laird and the lady could be so cruel.

"Och, the little dear!" Cook said. "I've no doubt ye would have—if ever ye'd had occasion to notice me, that is. Ye wouldna have been allowed to sit in the kitchen worritin' the maids with yer questions, that I promise you! Made to keep their distance from the servants, the young ladies of that house were, except to order us about. Ye'd have been a different person had ye grown up there, Miss Martha!"

Martha frowned. She did not understand how a house could make you a different person.

Cook had finished with the peas. Martha grabbed a last handful out of the bowl and ran outside to look for Duncan.

She found him down near the farmers' cottages, just beginning a game of Babylon with some of the tenant children.

"Miss Martha!" called Annie Davis. She was one of Sandy's daughters. She stood opposite Duncan on the grass, both of them holding their arms high and clasping hands to make an arch for the other children to walk through.

But when Annie saw Martha, she dropped Duncan's hands and said, "Ye must be Queen, Miss Martha."

"Nay, she's too little," said Annie's brother Johnny.

"I am not!" Martha cried indignantly, at the same time that Duncan said, "No, she isna!" Annie made a face at her brother and gestured for Martha to take her place opposite Duncan.

Martha stretched as tall as she could to make the arch with Duncan. Then Annie galloped underneath, and Martha and Duncan dropped their arms, trapping Annie between them.

Annie chanted the words of the game:

"How many miles to Babylon?"

Duncan and Martha chanted back:

"Threescore and ten."
"Will I be there by candlelight?"
"Yes, and back again."
"Open your gates and let me through!"
"Not without a beck and a boo!"

"There's your beck and there's your boo, Now open the gates and let me go through!"

As she said the last verse, Annie gave an imaginary coin to Duncan and to Martha, the King and Queen. They raised their arms again and let Annie gallop through. Then the next child in line came trotting up to the arch.

The game made the morning pass quickly, and before Martha knew it, it was dinnertime. The farmers' children all disappeared into their cottages for the meal, and Martha and Duncan raced up the hill to the Stone House. They must not be late for dinner.

If there was company, dinner was in the parlor. But on most days it was upstairs at the oak table in Mum and Father's bedroom. The bedroom was for eating in, and working in, and living in. It was there Mum sat to spin and tell stories after supper, or to sing the old songs she had learned when she was a little girl living far away beyond the mountains. It was there Father sat in his big chair and read from the books and newspapers that came by post from Edinburgh.

Alisdair read everything Father would let him. They would talk for hours about the new plows farmers were using in England, or about the trouble brewing in France, or about what was happening in America, the brand-new country across the sea where the people had fought a great war because they did not want to be ruled by the British king.

Martha liked to hear them talk about America best of all. Alisdair had told Martha that America had won its War for Independence in the year 1783, just one year after Martha was born. Martha had been spellbound—a whole country that was nearly the same age as a little girl! Why, Scotland was thousands of years old. She did not understand, exactly, how a country could be so young. Father said people had been living there long before it became a country. It was confusing, but still Martha liked to hear the stories.

Sometimes, at dinner, Father and Alisdair got carried away with talking. Then Mum would pick up a little silver bell and shake it at them to remind them they must eat as well as talk. Mollie would come racing up the stairs to see what her ladyship wanted, because the bell was supposed to mean something was needed from the kitchen.

"Can you serve up a dish of peace and quiet?" Mum would ask, smiling.

"Beggin' yer pardon, ma'am," Mollie would say, "it's only a housemaid I am, no a wisewoman who can make magic spells!"

"All right, all right," Father would growl in the voice that meant he was only pretending to be angry. "I'll keep to quiet topics for the rest of the meal."

But he always forgot. Cook complained that her fine cooking was wasted on a man like Father, who lived off words and ideas instead of bread and meat.

"I ought to cook up one of his great heavy books and serve it in a pie dish!" she grumbled. "Then happen he'd take note of what went into his mouth!"

So Mum kept ringing the bell to remind

Father to take bites now and then, and she made an agreement with Mollie.

"Never you mind running when you hear the bell," she said. "If it's you I'm wanting, I'll just bang a broomstick on the floor!"

Mollie said that suited her fine. Pounding was easier to listen for than the tinkling of the bell, anyway. Now a broomstick was always kept in the corner between the fireplace and Father's reading chair.

On the other side of the hearth was Father and Mum's huge four-poster bed with the green plaid curtains that hung all around it. The bed was so high that Mum had to use a little step stool to climb into it at night.

The oak dinner table was in the middle of the room, near the front windows. From her seat next to Grisie, Martha could look past Father's shoulders and see Loch Caraid shimmering at the foot of the hill. On a sunny day the water was the same deep blue as Mum's eyes. In cloudy weather it was bluish gray, like Father's.

At dinner that day, Father said he would go to look at his trees in the afternoon. In some fields on the west side of the valley he was raising hundreds of young trees from seed. Before Father, there had been hardly a single tree on the whole estate—only some twisted pines on the shoulders of the mountains, and a few fruit trees in the kitchen garden beside the house. Now there were two whole plantations of fir and larch.

Some people who did not know as much as Father did thought that the trees would be bad for the land. But Father knew better.

"You should see them, Margaret," he told Mum. "As tall as your waist now, and branching out splendidly. In another year we'll have quite a little wood down there." He broke off a piece of bread and, forgetting to eat it, waved it around as he talked.

"When those firs I put in behind the garden get big enough, you'll feel the difference. They'll break the wind in winter and shade us in the summer. I've half a mind to put in a row near the Tervish cottage. They feel the wind worse than we do."

Mum smiled at him. "It's a grand idea, Allan. But I thought Gavin Tervish was against the trees." Mr. Tervish was one of the farm-workers who rented land from Father. Martha liked him, with his great booming laugh and his flaming red hair that was even redder than Martha's and Alisdair's. But he was set in his ways and did not like it whenever Father instructed him to try something new.

"He is," Father said. "But now that he's a father, I'm thinking it's more worried he might be about the cold draughts whistling through the cracks in his walls."

Grisie gave a delighted gasp. "A father! Did Mrs. Tervish have the baby, then?"

Martha put down her fork, too excited to eat more. It was always grand news when a new baby was born on the estate. Mum was looking pleased, too. But Duncan, Alisdair, and Robbie went on shoveling food into their mouths as though Father had only said the Tervishes' cat had had kittens.

"Aye," Father said, looking surprised. "Did

I not mention it? A fine lad was born this morning before dawn, and both mother and bairn are doing fine. Auld Mary was there for the birthing, of course. I canna imagine how that woman kens when it's the right time."

"There's not much Auld Mary doesna ken," Mum said. "She has forgotten more than you or I will ever know." Martha knew Auld Mary was the old woman who lived away out on the moor, the great open stretch of land beyond the end of the lake. Auld Mary knew about every plant that grew and made potions and ointments for all the people of the valley. Whenever a baby was born, Auld Mary was there. She had been at Martha's own birth, though of course Martha did not remember it. Auld Mary had even been there when Father was born. She was a young woman then, but already she knew all about birthing bairns. It was said she had not missed any birth in the valley for more than fifty years.

Mum spooned up the last of her pudding and pushed the dish away from her. "Well!

We must get to work, girls. We'll have to fix up a basket of gifts for the bairn. I wasna expecting it quite so soon."

Grisie squeezed Martha's hand under the table. That meant they would pay the baby a visit tomorrow. Martha couldn't wait. There had not been a new baby in the valley in almost a year.

The New Bairn

The next morning, just before noon, Mum told Martha to change into her best dust-gown and to bring her brown hair ribbon to the bedroom. Mum gently gathered Martha's red curls and tied them away from her face. Then they set off for Gavin Tervish's cottage. Grisie walked slowly beside Mum, fresh and cool in her white muslin gown, with the basket of presents they had packed hanging over one arm. Martha ran ahead, leading the way down the hillside. They passed the cow-house, the stable, and the sheep-yard.

They passed the carriage-house and the mains, where the unmarried farmworkers lived. The men with families had their own cottages on the lakeshore, just down the hill and around the bend.

Like all the farmers' cottages, Gavin Tervish's was a long, narrow house built of turf, big squares of grass that had been cut from the moor and piled up one on top of the other like bricks. The roof was thatched with broom. Broom-grass was bunched into thick, watertight bundles and fastened onto the roof beams, and that was the thatch.

In the middle of the roof was a flat square of slate held up by four short legs. It looked like a little hat on top of the house. The slate covered a hole that had been made in the roof for smoke to come out, since there was no chimney. In bad weather rain could not beat in and put out the fire, because of the little slate hat.

There was no door, so the entrance was always open to the sun and wind. Martha could see inside to the round fireplace in the middle of the floor. Mrs. Tervish smiled at Martha from a seat near the fire. On her lap was a bundle of sheeting with a tuft of dark hair sticking out the top.

Martha liked the Tervish cottage, with its grass-covered earthen benches built right against the snug earthen walls and wisps of smoke weaving in and out of the blackened rafters overhead. The house was divided into three rooms by two inner walls. There was the tiny bedroom at one end, the kitchen in the middle, and a place for the cows at the other end. The inner walls did not go all the way to the roof, so that light and smoke could drift from one end of the house to the other. The strong smells of hay and cows drifted through, too.

Martha thought she would like to live in the same house with the cows, and listen to their soft noises at night. But Grisie said she was thankful Father's cows had their own house to live in. She would not like her clothes and hair to smell of cattle all the time.

The cows were out at pasture now because

it was daytime. Only Mrs. Tervish and the new baby were at home, and old Mrs. MacFarlane, who was Jeanie Tervish's mother. It was said she had had eleven children and had lost every one of them to sickness, except for Jeanie. There was a fierce, proud gleam in her eyes today as she sat hunched on a bench knitting rapidly and never looking away from her new grandson.

Mum and Grisie followed Martha into the cottage. Mrs. MacFarlane could hardly tear her eyes away from the bairn long enough to stand and nod a hello. But Mrs. Tervish greeted them warmly and began to rise, murmuring something about getting a cup of tea for her ladyship.

"Nonsense," Mum said, smiling. "You just sit you back down and rest. We didna come to make extra work for you, dear." Before Mrs. Tervish could say a thing, Mum had drawn a bench next to her chair and was cooing into the sheeting at the little red-faced baby.

"Such a fine young mannie he is," Mum said.

"Aye," said Mrs. Tervish in a soft voice, "he's a bonny one, he is."

"Jeanie Tervish!" said Mrs. MacFarlane in a shocked voice. "Mind yer tongue, lass! Do ye want to tempt the Wee Folk to steal your babe oot of yer varry arms?"

Without slowing a stitch in her knitting, the older woman rose and peered out the doorway. For a long moment she looked all around. Then she went back to her seat in the corner, shaking her head dourly.

"I didna see any fairies, but that doesn't mean there be none there. They'll snatch yer bairn quicker than a squirrel steals a nut, Jean Tervish, and leave ye with one of their own shriveled goblins, if ye gang on shoutin' to the warld how bonny he be." Her voice dropped to a whisper on the last words and she frowned fiercely at the baby, as if to scare his handsome looks away. But he did not look so very bonny to Martha. With his scrunched-up eyes and wrinkled red face he looked more like one of the changeling goblin babies Mrs. MacFarlane was worried about.

"Here now, I've a gift for his wee self," Mum said. She opened her purse and took out a silver coin. Mrs. Tervish nodded gratefully and unwrapped the bairn a bit to free a chubby hand. Mum gently opened the baby's fingers and placed the coin in his fist. He gripped it tightly for a moment, then waved his hand and let the coin fall to the ground.

"There now!" Mum said, pleased. "He'll grow to be a generous man. That's a grand sign, Jeanie."

Mrs. Tervish looked proud and happy. Martha knew that if the baby had held on to the coin, it would have meant he would grow up to be selfish and miserly. All new mothers were nervous when the first visitor placed the silver coin in the baby's hand. Martha wondered if she herself had dropped the coin when she was newly born. She hoped so. She would not like to be a mean, stingy woman when she grew up.

There were all kinds of precautions that must be taken with a new baby. No one must carry fire out of the house until the child was at least a week old. To do so would be very bad luck. So would speaking the name the child was to be given, until after he was christened. The minister himself must be the very first person to say the baby's name aloud. Mr. Tervish would have to write his son's name on a slip of paper and hand it to the minister just before the ceremony.

The wooden cradle at Mrs. Tervish's feet was borrowed. Even if the Tervishes had had a new cradle to give the bairn, it could not have been used last night. Only after the baby had had its first sleep in the borrowed cradle could it be given a new cradle of its own. And Mrs. Tervish was careful not to jostle the cradle with her feet, for it must never be rocked empty. Terrible things could happen if you were not careful. The fairies would carry off the baby—or worse, people said. But no one would tell Martha what the worse things might be.

Mum signaled to Grisie, and Grisie stepped forward shyly, carrying the basket. "We brought a few other tokens for the bairn," she said, setting the basket on the dirt floor beside Mrs. Tervish's chair.

"Och, 'tis far too kind ye are!" exclaimed Mrs. Tervish. "'Tis mair than enough ye came to see the child." She looked flustered and happy. Mrs. MacFarlane went on knitting and staring at her grandson, but her fierce expression had softened. Martha could see in her face how much she loved this wee, wrinkled baby and how pleased she was that he was receiving so much attention.

Mrs. Tervish looked at Grisie. "Happen ye'd like to hold him while I peek in yer basket?" she asked. But Grisie's eyes went wide with fear.

"Och, nay! He's such a tiny thing. I'm afraid I'd break him in two!"

"Well, I'm not," said Martha. "I'd like to hold him."

Mum laughed, and so did Mrs. Tervish. Grisie looked embarrassed, but Mrs. Tervish smiled at her.

"To be sure, I ken how ye feel, Miss Grisell," she said. "I did be thinkin' the same thing when Auld Mary put him in me arms yesterday mornin'. But once yer hands touch a bairn they seem to ken just what to do, all on their own."

"Aye," Mum put in. "I'll never forget how your father trembled the first time I held you out to him. Grown man that he was, he was that terrified his teeth were chattering! I had to make him sit down and hold you on his knees, like a cat. Even so, he shook so much, I began to worry he really might drop you on the flagstones and break you like an egg!"

Grisie was astonished. "Truly? Father was afraid?"

"That he was indeed. And he wept like a baby himself, when you opened your wee eyes and looked at him. Then I stopped worrying he'd drop you, and worried he'd drown you with his own tears instead!"

Everyone laughed at that, even old Mrs. MacFarlane. Martha could see by the twinkle in Mum's eye that she was exaggerating a little bit. But it was still funny to think of Father weeping like a baby.

"Aye, aye," cackled Mrs. MacFarlane, "and didna me son-in-law do the self-same thing! That great ox of a man, wailin' like a young lassie with a broken heart. Dinna ye worrit yerself, Miss Grisie. Ye'll ken what to do when the time comes—and do it a sight better than any overgrown babe of a man!"

Grisie blushed, but she was still giggling.

"Please might I hold him?" Martha said impatiently. She didn't know what Mrs. MacFarlane meant about "the time coming" or why Grisie blushed, and she didn't want to know. She wanted to hold the baby.

"Sit yourself down here, young miss." Mum patted the bench beside her. "Is it all right with you, Jeanie?"

"Of course, Lady Glencaraid," Mrs. Tervish said. Carefully she placed the bairn in Martha's outstretched arms, and Mum showed Martha how to steady the baby's head and neck with one arm while the other arm kept snug under his little body. He squirmed and fussed for just a moment and then gave a little sigh and settled deeper into sleep.

Martha stared down at his head with its tiny smudge of a nose and the perfect little red bow of his mouth. She wondered how on earth she could ever have thought he was a changeling baby.

Mrs. Tervish slowly unpacked the basket of gifts. Wrapped in a fine linen napkin were a dozen currant cakes and beneath them a large wedge of cheese. Cook had fretted all morning about those cakes as she bustled about the kitchen mixing and baking.

"Och, I might have guessed her ladyship would be wantin' sweeties for the bairn," she had grumbled. "As if the child could eat them, a day old as it is! Gang straight down the gullet of Gavin Tervish himself, they will, and what that great lug of a man needs with currant cakes is beyond me. But there," she said, sighing and wiping floury hands on her apron, "her ladyship has that soft a heart that she'll use up all her nice currant jam on a tenant."

"But Cook," Martha had said, "we have plenty of currant jam! There are four jars more in the bedroom closet. You made them your-self." There was a special shelf in Mum's big closet for the household jams and jellies and spices. Martha had counted the squat jars full of bright red jam lined up on the shelf this morning, when Mum gave her one to take down to Cook.

Cook raised her eyebrows. "So, it's Lady Martha I'll have to be callin' ye from noo on, is it? Takin' such an interest in the household stores as you are. And has yer fine mither given over the keys to you, then?"

Martha had laughed, for she knew Cook wasn't really cross. It was just her way to scold and fuss. She was very proud of her currant cakes and was pleased that Mum thought them fine enough for a gift—even if Cook did think they were too fine a gift for a cottager's bairn.

Beneath the cakes and cheese was a bottle of home-brewed ale for the new father, and a soft woollen blanket woven of thread Mum had spun herself. It was fine, thin, strong thread that made a cloth as soft as a kitten's fur. Mrs. Tervish shook her head admiringly.

"Ye have but to look at it to see who had the spinning of it," she said. "But, ma'am, it's far too fine for the likes of—"

"Nonsense," Mum interrupted. She hated such talk. So did Martha. She did not like to think of the estates where the laird treated his servants and tenants poorly, like the one Cook had lived on. Cook had told her that some of the cottagers on that estate had been afraid to build too warm a fire even in winter, for fear the laird would think they were getting to be too well off and would raise the rents. And Alisdair said that many lairds were forcing all the tenant farmers to move off their land in order to turn the land over to sheep farming. A laird could make more money raising sheep than by renting land to farmers.

But that was no excuse, Father said, to rob people of their livelihood and kick them out of their homes. For many years Father had worked hard to bring better ways of farming to his land, so that the people who had lived and worked there so long might keep their homes and improve their lot in life. Martha agreed with Father. She knew that if she were a laird, she'd not let her cottagers go hungry, nor their wee bairns like the one in her arms.

After a while the baby began to fuss. Mrs. Tervish said he was hungry and took him back so she could feed him. Mum rose and said it was time to be going, for Cook would have dinner waiting. Martha hated to leave. But outside, on the way back along the lake path, Mum took a napkin-wrapped bundle out of her pocket and handed it to Grisie. Inside were three little golden cakes, glistening with ruby jam.

"Currant cakes!" Martha cried. "You saved us some!"

Grisie gave one to Martha and one to Mum. They walked slowly up the path, eating the cakes. Grisie liked the cake part best, and Mum liked the jam. But Martha liked the way the tastes of sweet cake and tart jam mixed in her mouth. When she had licked the last of the jam from her fingers, she wiped her hands on her dust-gown and ran the rest of the way up the hill. A little wind came tickling up behind her as if it wanted to race, and it carried with it Mum's laugh and Grisie's soft voice, and the splashing of the lake water upon the shore. Martha thought of the tiny bairn she had held in the cottage. It had never yet felt the wind or seen the lake or tasted a currant cake. Martha was glad she was a girl getting bigger every day, and not a baby anymore.

The Brownie

The next day it was raining, and then it rained all day, every day, for a week. The first day Father was pleased. He said the rain had come just when he was beginning to worry that the summer would be too dry to bring in a good crop. But after the fifth day of steady pounding rain he began to wear his stern look, and he did not talk much. This rain was not the ordinary drizzle of a Highland evening; it was heavy and cold, and it beat at the green blades in the fields. Mum told Martha a wet summer could be worse than a summer that was too dry.

"But do not you fret yourself about it," she said. "'Tis no use stewing about things you canna alter."

Martha could not help but fret a little. She was tired of staying in the house all the time.

Then one morning when Martha woke up, Mollie was already in the room, dishing out the porridge. She said the sun was shining with all its might.

Martha was glad, and she danced a little dance on the floorboards. But Mollie said, "Och, I'd tread lightly today if I was ye, Miss Martha. Cook's in a fearful dark mood and I doubt her poor nerves can take a pounding from the ceiling."

"What's wrong?" Martha asked.

Mollie looked grave, and her voice was nearly a whisper. "Forgot to leave the brownie his supper last night, she did."

"She never!" gasped Grisie. Martha could only stare. In all her life she had never known Cook to do such a thing.

Duncan and Robbie came out from behind

the dressing-screen. They wanted to know what was wrong, and when they heard, they could not believe their ears.

A brownie was a tiny, tiny man who lived in someone's house and did little chores if he was left bits of food, and played tricks if he was not. Cook said the Stone House brownie was named Tullie Grayshanks. She said he had moved in as soon as the last slate was put on the roof, and he had been there ever since. He scared hawks away from the hens and made sure the foolish hens didn't lay eggs outside the chicken-house. If a button or needle was lost in the house, he'd find it and leave it where someone would be sure to see it. Cook said he helped herd sheep, cut hay, thresh oats, and do all sorts of other things around the farm. No one had ever seen him do those things, but Cook said he was there doing them just the same, and if you paid attention you would see that there was always more hay stacked than the farmers had cut.

Martha had hunted all over the house, but she had never seen Tullie Grayshanks. Cook said he was twelve inches high and wore a little ragged suit of brown clothes. He had a pointed beard and glittering black eyes. Martha had searched behind every cabinet and peered inside every mousehole, but Tullie must always have heard her coming.

Every night Cook put out a little dish of cream and a round cake of oat bread called a bannock. She left them by the kitchen door and they were always gone the next morning. She said brownies were sensitive things and you had to be very careful not to upset them.

"Ye must nivver offer him his meat and drink directly," she had told Martha. "If once ye do, he'll gang away and nivver come back. And ye must nivver take him for granted, either. I've heard o' one brownie who worked in a house a hundred years, and then one day the housewife chanced to say that the brownie was such a great help she had it in mind to let the kitchenmaid go. Snick-snack, oot the door the brownie went and nivver was he seen on that farm again."

But the worst thing that could happen was for someone to make the brownie angry. Then the brownie would turn into a boggart, and he would play terrible tricks all over the farm. He would tie up the horses' manes in knots, and he'd make their horseshoes fall off. He would stop the hens from laying eggs and the cows from giving milk. He would creep into the kitchen and set the fire roaring so high that the bannocks would burn, or he would make it burn so low that the broth would never boil. There was no end to the mischief a boggart could do, when he was of a mind to.

Cook said one sure way to offend a brownie was to forget to leave him his supper. And now she had gone and done just that!

"Is Tullie Grayshanks angry, then?" Duncan asked.

"'Tis no for me to say," Mollie said. "But when Cook woke up this mornin' all the milk in the dairy was curdled. And not only that— yer mither's good china platter was lyin' smashed on the parlor floor, sure as I live."

"The brownie did that?" Martha wasn't sure

she wanted to go downstairs, if there was an angry brownie about.

Mollie shook her head. "I canna say. It could be that I stood the platter wrong on the shelf when I put it away last night. Happen it tipped off balance and fell in the night. I canna blame the brownie when just as likely it was me own fault. 'Tis that sorry I am, too, for that platter cost a shilling and 'twill mean no new winter dress for me if I'm to pay it off. But Cook says no one can blame me for curdlin' the milk, and she says she ought to pay for the platter, as it's her what riled up the brownie."

Alisdair slid open the door of his bed. "I dinna believe there is any brownie," he said in his matter-of-fact way. "That's just a story for children."

"Alisdair!" Martha cried, shocked.

Duncan said, "Then who eats the bannocks every night?"

"One o' the sheepdogs, most likely," Alisdair said. "They're always roaming about at night. And I should think it's the barn cats that drink up the cream."

"Whisht!" scolded Mollie. "Mind yer tongue, Master Alisdair. No one can stop ye from havin' such thoughts in yer head, but if ye're wrong ye might rile him all the more—and wi' us halfway to havin' a boggart on our hands as it is!"

Alisdair shrugged. He never minded if people did not agree with his ideas.

"What will we do if Tullie goes on being angry, Mollie?" Martha asked.

"Och, there's no tellin'. I've heard o' people driven from their homes by boggarts. But Cook is downstairs now, mixin' and stirrin' for all she's worth. She aims to leave him some special little cakes wi' his cream tonight. She says happen Tullie will forgive her, seein' as it's the first and only time she's ever forgotten him, and that only because she had such a fearful headache last night she could scarce remember her own name!"

Martha hoped Cook's plan would work. She did not want to have to leave the Stone House. But she did not want to live with a boggart, either. Auld Mary told stories about the things boggarts could do. In one house the boggart made himself invisible and sat down beside the laird at dinner every day. The boggart ate up most of the laird's food, but the laird never knew it. He only knew that he began every meal with a plate full of food and finished with an empty one, yet he was as hungry as if he'd eaten no more than a bite or two. In time he grew so thin that one day a great gust of wind blew him off his horse and carried him all the way to England. Martha did not want that to happen to Father.

The porridge wasn't very good this morning. Cook had put in neither sugar nor salt. Martha ate as much as she could stand and then Grisie helped her get dressed. Martha took Lady Flora and went down to the kitchen to see if she could help make the cakes. Duncan came, too.

"Happen she'll let us lick the spoon!" he said.

But Cook hardly glanced at them when they came into the room. She was beating eggs in a bowl, stirring so fast and so hard that her knuckles were white on the spoon. Her mouth was set in a thin, worried line.

"Good morning to you," said Martha, feeling rather shy.

"Ye may call it that if you like," Cook answered crisply, not looking up from her bowl.

Martha and Duncan looked at each other. Duncan's eyes said to Martha, *Let's go out to the garden instead.*

Aye, let's, Martha's eyes replied.

Almost tiptoeing, they went through the kitchen and out the back door. Nannie was sitting on a little stool just outside the open doorway, peeling potatoes. She was a short, plump, golden-haired girl with teasing eyes and a round face. She was very shy and quiet around Mum or Father, but when she was alone with Mollie or Cook she never stopped laughing. Her father was another tenant farmer, like Mr. Tervish. Nannie had seven brothers and sisters who lived in one of the little two-room cottages by the lake with Nannie's parents and their cows. Nannie was the oldest.

She said she never minded how much work she had to do in a day, for it was so nice to sleep in the attic with just Mollie instead of sharing a bed with her four sisters.

"Feel like a grand lady meself, I do, lying there wi' no one's elbows in me ribs!" she had told Martha once.

Today she said, "I'd stay clear of the kitchen this mornin', if I were ye. Cook's that out o' sorts, she doesna ken what she's sayin'."

"Aye," Martha agreed, and Duncan nodded his head. Martha stood a moment feeling the warm sun on her skin. The garden was a soft, wet, glittering world of green and silver. Sunbeams melted on the whitewashed stone walls of the dairy, the little low building just behind the Stone House. The dairy was where the milk and butter were kept and where the churning was done. It was always dark and cool inside. Sometimes Martha and Duncan played that the dairy was a cave, and they were famous outlaws like Rob Roy MacGregor, who had lived many years ago in the next county over. But today Martha didn't want to play indoors.

Duncan went to pick some plums from the trees at the edge of the garden. Martha followed him slowly, feeling the mud squelch between her toes. The kitchen garden was enclosed by low stone walls and ringed with rows of pear and apple trees. It was laid on a flattish part of the hill, where the slope was very gentle. At the far end, helping to block the winds that swept down off the mountain, was a line of buildings: the alehouse, the laundry, and the dovecote, where pigeons were raised. The pigeons made a constant cooing noise that was like water rushing over stones. Martha could hear them now, adding their murmur to the chattering of the wrens and finches who fluttered among the fruit trees.

Tiny green balls hung thick on the apple trees. Martha wished they would hurry and get ripe. The plums were ripe and heavy on the branches, though, so Martha took a plum from Duncan and ate it instead as she wandered around the garden. She liked to tickle her fingers on the feathery tops of the carrots and parsnips. The baby lettuces and spinach plants in the salad patch seemed twice as big as when she had seen them a week ago. There was watercress, too, and chervil and chicory and asparagus. Sandy did most of the work in the kitchen garden, and he had taught Martha the names of everything that grew there.

She stooped to peek at the cucumbers growing under their broad, flat leaves. She had heard Sandy tell Cook that he was worried the cucumbers would rot away with all the rain. But they looked all right to Martha.

There was one little cucumber that had broken off of its vine. Martha wiped off the mud on her dust-gown and made the cucumber Lady Flora's horse, and the garden a valley where Lady Flora lived. Lady Flora's painted wooden face smiled up at Martha. She was a very special doll, and there was not another like her in all of Glencaraid. Father had brought her all the way from Edinburgh when he had traveled there last year. She had dark glass eyes and rosy cheeks. Fluffy golden curls peeked out from beneath her little lace cap.

Martha helped Lady Flora gallop around her estate to look things over just as Father did. Duncan had climbed into the plum tree and was quietly eating plums one after the other, with his brows drawn together in the same way that Father's looked when he was writing an important letter. Martha galloped over to him to get another plum. Then she galloped to the herb patch to get some tansy flowers for Lady Flora's hair. She liked to break off bits of the different herbs to smell them. Her favorite was the sweet smell of mint, but thyme was nice, too, with its fresh lemony scent, and there were the spicy smells of sage and tansy and pennyroyal, and the rosemary that smelled like wind in a fir grove.

Thunk. Thunk. Duncan was throwing plum pits at the stone wall. He jumped down from the tree and lined some pits up on top of the wall, and then tried to knock them off with another pit.

"Let me try," Martha said. She set the cucumber horse to graze in a patch of tansy and put Lady Flora carefully down beside it.

She and Duncan took turns throwing, but the pits were small and very hard to hit.

"Happen we could use *her* for a target," Duncan said, pointing at Lady Flora sleeping in the tansy patch.

"Nay! You'd better not—" Martha began, outraged, but then Duncan flashed her a grin and she saw that he was teasing.

"Let's use her horse," she said.

They threw pits at the cucumber until all the pits were lost over the wall and the poor horse fell off too. It was so pleasant in the sunny garden with Duncan that Martha almost forgot how upside-down things were inside the house. It was strange to think of Cook working furiously inside, worrying all the time about Tullie Grayshanks.

A hawk circled overhead and Martha felt a sudden pang of fear for the little chicks in the hen-yard, on the other side of the garden wall. Who would look out for them if Tullie Grayshanks did not? Martha wished she could talk to him and tell him not to be angry with Cook. It was not Cook's fault she had had a bad headache last night. Martha had not even known Cook was feeling unwell. That was another strange thing to think about. While she had been upstairs in Father and Mum's bedroom yesterday evening, laughing and feeling happy, Cook had been downstairs with a sick headache.

"Yah, yah, go away, you auld hawk!" Martha yelled into the sky.

Duncan laughed. "He's no after the chicks, you goose," he said. "He's after mice in the oat field."

But Martha yelled again, "Yah, go on with you, hawk!" She held up Lady Flora and made her yell "Yah, yah!" too.

If the hawk heard them, he did not show it. He went on soaring in lazy circles, thinking his own private hawk thoughts.

After a while Mum walked out through the garden, with barley cakes and cold sliced chicken and a big tumbler of milk for Martha and Duncan to share.

"Your father is dining at South Loch today," she explained. "Wants to see how the rains have hit the oats there, he does. So I told poor Cook not to worry about a big dinner for the rest of us."

The children sat on a garden bench beside Mum to eat their dinner. Mum leaned back against the stone wall and closed her eyes. The breeze made little curls flutter on her neck and forehead. Martha thought there could not be any nicer way to eat, sitting here with Duncan and Mum and Lady Flora in the sunny garden corner. For a moment she felt almost glad that Cook was so out of sorts that they had to eat outdoors—but not really glad. She didn't want Cook to be unhappy.

"Will Cook or Mollie have to pay for your platter?" she asked.

"Nay," Mum said. "I'll no take money out o' their pockets. 'Twas no one's fault it fell. Happen someone slammed a door too hard and it made the cabinet shake. Who can say?"

"Or happen the brownie did it?"

"Aye, happen so."

"Will the brownie forgive Cook, after he eats her cakes tonight?" Martha asked.

Mum smiled. "Wouldna you?"

Duncan grinned and wiped milk off his mouth. "I would, sure as day!"

Martha thought of Cook's delicious cakes. "Aye," she said. "That I would."

She knew then that it would be all right. Tullie Grayshanks would not turn into a boggart, nor would he leave Glencaraid. He would know Cook was sorry and would never forget him again. Martha wondered if perhaps Cook would help her to make a little cake for the brownie, so that she could make friends with him. She would like to see him. It was nice to have a brownie around the house, to find buttons and watch out for the chickens and keep Cook company in the lonely downstairs late at night.

Overhead the hawk wheeled and flapped his great wings and soared away until he was lost in the endless sky.

The Christening

One night Mum said the next day was Sunday and that it would be a kirk day, a church day. The whole family must get up early to go to Clachan, the little village across the lake. Father had arranged for the ferryman to carry them, for they would not all fit in the little rowboat. Martha was excited about the trip. The last time there had been a kirk day, she had not known about the water fairy. This time she would keep a sharp eye out and perhaps she would see the beautiful lady with the long green hair.

The kirk in Clachan held services only once a month. The trip was too long to make more often than that. On the other Sundays Father read aloud from the big Bible in the parlor, and he said a lot of prayers before dinner. Sometimes it was hard to sit still and be solemn when the smell of Cook's good roast mutton was wafting down from the head of the table. Martha liked kirk days better, for then all the prayers were said in the kirk, and when her family went to the minister's house for dinner he said only one little short prayer before carving the meat. Mum said that was the sign of a man with a True Understanding of Human Nature. Martha did not know what that meant, but she was glad the minister had it. After the long sermon in the kirk, she was always very hungry.

But today was not a usual kirk day. The Tervish baby was going to be christened. Instead of dinner at the minister's house, there would be a big feast on the grass outside the church after the morning service. Cook had been up since three in the morning, baking.

The Christening

Nearly everyone on the estate was going.

The sun had not yet begun to peek over the eastern hills when Father opened the front door and called out for everyone to make ready to leave. Grisie hastily finished smoothing Martha's curls over the shoulders of her white muslin dress. Today Martha did not have to wear a dust-gown. But she mustn't get even the tiniest spot on her best Sunday dress, and that meant she couldn't run and play with Duncan and the village children after the christening.

Mum was beautiful in her buttercup-yellow silk with the lacy, trailing elbow-sleeves and the gauze-trimmed flounces. Martha liked the way Mum's skirt swung gently back and forth when she walked, making shadows chase each other across the silk. Grisie wore a silk dress, too, a rose-colored one that had belonged to Mum when she was a girl. With her pink cheeks and shining hair, Grisie was almost as pretty as Lady Flora. Martha had wanted to bring Lady Flora today, too, but Mum said she had better stay home.

The boys were stiff and awkward in their crisp white linen shirts, blue breeches, and scarlet vests and coats. Their hair had been brushed smooth and neat before they left the house, although the wind had already rumpled Alisdair's red mane into its usual tousled waves. Martha thought they all looked very fine, even rumple-haired Alisdair.

But Father was the finest of all. He had put on the clothes that belonged to a true Highland laird. He wore a coat of tartan plaid over his linen shirt. A wide piece of tartan cloth was belted around his waist and looped over his shoulder. This was called his kilt, and Mum had spun every bit of the thread herself. His jacket had gold buttons and wide, turned-back cuffs lined with silk. Red-and-black tartan stockings came up to his knees, and at the top of each was a golden tassel. On his head he wore his bonnet, a large brimless hat with a knot of black ribbon tied round it.

He stood in the yard, looking down the hill toward the lake. A pale light was beginning to show at the corners of the sky. The air was quiet and still; there was no wind this morning. The valley was hushed, half asleep.

Then, so gently that Martha could not tell at exactly what moment it began, there came a high, sweet, reedy note, like someone singing. It swelled and grew louder, and then the note went higher and lower and became a song. The sound was soft and sharp at the same time. It made Martha shiver. It was like the valley had found a voice and begun to sing.

It was the sound of bagpipes, and it grew louder and nearer. Sandy was playing, down by the lakeshore at the cluster of huts. Today he was not Father's steward—he was Father's piper. There had been a time when no Highland laird would have gone anywhere, even across his own estate, without his piper behind him. But times had changed, and the old ways were fading. Today, though, was a special day. A christening was a time for celebration, and for piping.

The pipes grew louder, and soon Martha could see the shapes of Sandy and his family coming up the path. Behind them were Mr.

and Mrs. Tervish and old Mrs. MacFarlane. Mr. Tervish held the baby in his arms. He looked as proud as if he were a laird himself.

Behind the Tervishes came the rest of the farmers and their families, and all the servants who worked on the home farm. As soon as they reached the Stone House they would all have to turn around again and walk back down to the lake, where the ferry would be waiting. But the new bairn's first journey must be uphill, for good luck, and so he was brought to the Stone House first. When Mr. Tervish reached the house, he bowed to Father and Mum. Then he turned and held the baby up so his little eyes could see the lake. The water was shot with streaks of fire now, for the sun was rising. Martha could see the dark shape of the ferryman's boat down on the water.

No one spoke as Father led the way down the hill to the shore. Sandy's piping soared above their heads. Martha thought there was no sound in the world she liked better than bagpipes, except, perhaps, Mum's laugh.

At the shore the ferryman bowed to Father and Mum. His name was Mr. Shaw. His hair was long and shaggy, and his sleeves were rolled up over his strong arms.

"Sit ye right here, miss," he said to Martha, helping her to a seat in the middle of the boat. A rug was spread on the boards to protect her dress. Grisie sat down next to her. The boat rocked from side to side as the boys clambered aboard.

"Are you boys or cattle, then?" Mum laughed. "Tread a bit lighter, lads."

When the whole family was seated, the ferryman gave a great shove with his pole and the boat surged away from the shore. Martha waved at the group of cottagers and servants left behind. The ferry would come back for them after it left the Morses on the opposite shore. It would have to make three or four trips to carry such a crowd. A kirk day meant a lot of work for the ferryman.

Sandy's piping seemed to speed the boat across the water. To the west the mountains stood tall and velvety green. Martha could see a curve of the road high above the water, like a bit of ribbon cresting the folds of a green dress. On the other side of the lake, far to the east, the gray shape of the rocky hill called the Creag was shrouded in mist. Mist curled above the water, too, in strange, dancing figures.

Martha remembered to look for the water fairy. For a moment she thought she could see strands of green hair floating in the water just ahead, but the boat moved closer and she saw it was only a willow branch with long, pale leaves.

"Martha!" Mum said. "You know better than to hang over the boat like that. Do you fancy a swim, in your good dress?"

Martha sat back down but she did not stop looking. She turned her head to search the water on one side of the boat and then the other, until Father said she looked like a weathercock in a windstorm. Then Sandy's bagpipes, fainter now, took up the notes of a psalm Martha knew well, and Robbie and Duncan began to sing in loud voices.

The Christening

Martha sighed. The fairy would hear them coming and hide for certain. She gave up searching and sang along with the boys, instead. It was Sunday and so they must sing only hymns, but God didn't mind if they sang them loudly.

"Fire warnings and hymn singing, that's what He made shouts for," Father said.

The sun rose higher and burned off the mist. The water of Loch Caraid now shone green as a water fairy's hair. Larks wheeled overhead in the pale-blue sky. The shore grew closer and closer until *bump!* the boat knocked against the grassy bank. Mr. Shaw leaped nimbly out of the boat and secured it to a wooden post sunk into the ground. He held out a hand to help Mum step onto the shore. Father picked Martha up and lifted her out of the boat.

"There you be, Light-as-a-Feather! Mind your shoes don't get wet!"

Martha's toes squirmed inside her boots.

She wished she were not wearing them at all. Kirk days were the only days all summer when she had to wear shoes and stockings. She didn't like to wear them even in winter, and would run barefoot over the frosty ground until Mum or Grisie caught her.

Father said they would wait at the shore for the carriage. He had arranged for one of his men to drive it around the lake and pick them up for the three-mile ride to Clachan. While they waited, Mum passed around bread and cheese for everyone to eat. They had not eaten breakfast before leaving home. Martha nibbled on her bannock and watched the ferry glide across the water, back to the Glencaraid side.

Then Mum said she had a surprise for Grisie. "Save a bit of that cheese and bread," she said. "Jeannie Tervish asked if you'd carry the bairn to the kirk."

"Me?" Grisie gasped.

Mum laughed. "Aye. I confess I was expecting it. You know the bairn must go to kirk in the arms of an unmarried lass. 'Twill bring luck to the babe if that girl is his laird's daughter."

Grisie's eyes shone. "I never thought about it," she said.

"I thought you were afraid to hold a bairn," Martha said. She felt a little disappointed, although she had not remembered either that someone would be chosen to carry the bairn.

"I'm not afraid. I was just caught by surprise that other time." Grisie tossed her head. "But Mum—how shall I carry the bread and cheese? I've no pockets in this dress!" Martha knew that was part of the tradition. The girl who held the bairn must carry with her something to eat, which she had to give to the first man she met along the way.

"Wrap them in a pocket-handkerchief and pin them to your skirt," Alisdair suggested.

"Tie them to your head," said Robbie.

"Aye, with your hair ribbon!" Duncan added. The boys burst out laughing. Martha laughed, too, to think of Grisie walking into the kirk in her pretty silk dress with a hunk of cheese and a bannock of bread tied to her head like a hat.

Grisie swept them a disdainful glance. Mum said, "The bairn will be in a basket. You can just tuck the bread and cheese right alongside it."

"Ah! Here's the carriage," Father said. Martha heard its wheels bumping before she saw it. Then it came around the bend, a small open carriage pulled by Father's two shaggy mountain ponies. "Who wants to ride?"

Martha and Duncan looked at each other. It was hard to choose. Father did not take his carriage out often, and a ride in it was a special treat. But it would be great fun to walk the road to Clachan with the Tervishes and Sandy and Cook and the rest.

"We can ride home," Duncan said.

Martha nodded. "Aye. May we walk, Father?"

"As you wish," Father said. "But you're not to dawdle along the way. I'll not have you come late to kirk."

"And 'walk' means walk," Mum put in. "No berry-picking, no footraces, and"—she looked hard at Martha—"no stains of any kind on your nice clean clothes!"

"Yes, ma'am," Martha mumbled.

"What for the rest of you?" Father asked. "Robert? Coming with us, I suppose?"

"Aye!" Robbie said. He rode in the carriage every chance he got.

"I'll walk, Father," said Alisdair.

Biting her lip, Grisie looked down at her dainty slippers and her smooth, neat hem. "I suppose I ought to walk too, if I'm to hold the bairn," she said doubtfully. The road would be dusty and her shoes were sure to get scuffed. It was another thing about shoes that did not make sense to Martha. Either they were big and heavy and hot, so that the poor feet were miserable inside them, or they were so light and pretty that walking any distance at all would ruin them. Martha wondered who had invented them, and whether his friends had still liked him afterward.

"You needn't carry the bairn the whole way, Grisie. Only the last bit and into kirk," Mum reminded her. "Why don't you ride with us as far as the bridge, and you can wait there for the rest to catch up?"

Grisie smiled, relieved. "Aye, that suits me. Alisdair, you'll explain to Mrs. Tervish?"

Almost as soon as the carriage had rumbled away with Father, Mum, Grisie, and Robbie, the ferryman's boat returned. Gavin Tervish stepped out of the boat and lifted a rather noisy basket onto the ground. Martha rushed forward to peek inside. The baby, well wrapped in the blanket Mum had given him, was waving his little fists in the air and screaming with all his might. He looked so angry and helpless, with his red face and toothless gums, that Martha longed to pick him up. She wished Mrs. Tervish had asked her to carry him to the christening. After all, she was an unmarried girl, too!

"Not much of a sailor, is he?" said Mr. Tervish.

Mrs. Tervish hurried ashore and lifted the crying child out of the basket, nestling him into her arms. "Hush, now, me liddle man. Whisht! There did be no more rocking in that boat than in yer own nice cradle, so never ye mind yer fussin' . . ." Her voice was soft and crooning. The baby calmed and snuggled against his mother.

The rest of the passengers were out of the boat now: Mrs. MacFarlane, Sandy, Mrs. Sandy, and Cook, Mollie, and Nannie. Mrs. Sandy was really Mrs. Davis, but everyone called her by her husband's first name so as not to confuse her with her sister-in-law, who had married Sandy's older brother and was also Mrs. Davis. Mrs. Sandy was a short, stout woman with untidy hair and very neat clothes. She had a way of always putting her hands on her hips when she spoke, so that whatever she said seemed like something quite important, even if it was just "Would ye like a bannock?" or "The water is boiling." Martha liked her very much.

"Miss Martha!" said Mrs. Sandy, hands on hips. "It's taller you're getting every day."

"Yes, ma'am." Martha felt as though she must work a little harder at growing, since it pleased Mrs. Sandy so much.

"And Master Duncan," Mrs. Sandy continued, "you're looking well."

Duncan gave a nervous kind of laugh and brushed a lock of hair off his forehead. If Mrs. Sandy said you were looking well, you felt somehow as though you had better not disappoint her.

When the baby was settled, Mrs. Tervish tucked him back into the basket, saying, "Shall we be off, then?" Mr. Shaw had gone back for another load of passengers, but Mrs. Sandy said they needn't wait.

"It's mostly my brood, and sure they ken their way to Clachan well enough!"

And so, with a lot of chatter and laughter, the party set off along the dirt path toward the village. It was a three-mile walk through a steep green valley. The stream that ran out of Loch Caraid traveled alongside the road, bubbling over stones on its way to Loch Earn, the big lake just south of Clachan. Sheep wandered about on the lush hillsides. They were Father's sheep, and they were looking fat and content with the summer's good grazing.

Before she had walked half a mile, Martha's feet began to throb in protest. Mum had said she must not run or stain her dress, but she hadn't mentioned keeping her boots on. Martha knelt down and wrestled them off. Then, ignoring Cook's raised eyebrows, she slid off her stockings and stuffed them into her boots. She would put them back on at the bridge leading into town, she decided.

After that the walk passed quickly. It seemed like no time at all before Martha spotted the footbridge. Beyond it, across the stream, rose the steeple of the little kirk in the village. Clachan was a small town, with only four shops plus the school and the kirk, but it seemed very large to Martha. There were twenty or more houses and a wide street running from one end of the town to the other.

"Look at her there, like a great pink rose," Mrs. Sandy murmured to Cook. Martha looked where she was pointing and saw Grisie waiting beneath a tree beside the bridge. Grisie looked so pretty and grown-up that for a moment Martha hardly recognized her sister. With her fine gown and the straight, delicate way she held herself, Grisie looked every bit as much a lady as Mum. Mrs. Sandy strode forward to greet her. Martha quietly stepped aside to put her boots and stockings back on. Mollie helped her with the buckles.

"Did Alisdair explain that I'd be waiting here?" Grisie asked Mrs. Tervish anxiously.

"Aye, that he did, and a sensible plan it was. Gowns like that wasna made for traipsin' through the bracken." Mrs. Tervish looked admiringly at Grisie's dress.

"This is the bread and cheese?" Mrs. Sandy asked, nodding at a napkin-wrapped bundle in Grisie's hand.

"Aye," Grisie said. Mrs. Sandy took the bundle and placed it in the basket at the baby's feet. Then she put her hands on her hips and told Grisie she must not speak another word until they reached the kirk. And she must give the bread and cheese to the first man she met, no matter who it was.

"But dinna ye speak to him," warned Mrs. Sandy, "or ye'll bring ill luck upon the child."

Grisie nodded, looking as if she wished she'd never left home. But she held out her arm for the basket, and when she peeked in at the sleeping bairn, she smiled. Martha wished she had something to do, to help make the baby's life lucky.

Grisie led the way across the bridge into Clachan. Close behind her, Martha's feet made clomping noises on the stones. The little crowd of churchgoers followed in a quietly chattering parade. Grisie was the only one who must not speak. Martha drew up beside her and talked and talked, because it was so funny to say things to Grisie when she couldn't answer back.

"I wonder what they'll name the bairn?" she said. "If I were a boy, they could name him after me." Grisie shot her a scornful look, but said nothing. Martha ignored her. "I suppose they could name him Martin, and that would be sort of like my name."

"Nay," said Duncan from behind. "They ought to call him Duncan, for me."

"You don't care a whit about bairns," Martha said. "He ought to be named for someone who appreciates him. Or else after one of his grandfathers dead and gone."

"What were their names?" Duncan asked.

"I dinna ken. Una Shaw's grandfather is called Whiskers. I think that's a fine name." Una Shaw was the ferryman's daughter.

Grisie opened her mouth to retort and snapped it shut just in time. She glared at Martha.

"Miss Martha, Master Duncan—ye're no pesterin' yer sister, are ye?" Cook called. "Ye mustn't distract her into speakin', ye ken."

"Och, nay, Cook," Martha said. " 'Tis just keepin' her company we are."

Grisie rolled her eyes, but she could not say otherwise. Martha giggled. Perhaps it was not so bad that Grisie had been chosen to carry the bairn, after all.

They had walked halfway through town. The kirk was just at the end of the road. Father's carriage stood outside, and there was a great crowd of people at the door. Martha wondered how Grisie would decide which of them was the first man she met. They were crowded together and she would reach them all at once.

They passed the weaver's shop and the smithy. Mrs. Tervish hovered close behind Grisie. Martha's stomach fluttered excitedly.

Suddenly Martha realized there was a new noise mixed in with the noise of the crowd, a sound that should not be there. It was a great baaing and bleating that got louder and louder until it was louder than the people's voices. It was a flock of sheep!

"What in the world?" Mrs. Sandy declared. Martha knew what she meant. What were sheep doing in the middle of town on a Sunday? It was not a market day.

Sheep began to amble out of a lane between two houses. Behind the houses was open pasture land and that was where they had come from. The noisy flock came trotting out from the lane and filled the road right in front of Grisie. Grisie's mouth was wide open but she remembered not to speak. The sheep filed around her, taking no notice of Grisie or the baby in the basket on her arm. Martha dodged out of the way of a large ewe who wanted to cross right where she was standing. Duncan was laughing and so were a lot of the people gathered on the kirk steps. It was so funny to see the indifferent sheep with their coats dirty from a summer on the hillsides, milling around the party of churchgoers dressed in their finest clothes.

"Get ye off me foot, ye witless beastie!" Gavin Tervish's booming voice called. "In heaven's name, who's got the keepin' of these sheep?"

"I do," said a cheerful voice. "Sure and they're the luckiest sheep in all Scotland, for I am their master!"

Martha knew that voice. It belonged to the little man who was suddenly standing right in front of Grisie. Martha had not seen him walk into the road. It was as if he had popped out of nowhere, like one of the Wee Folk.

Indeed, he looked like one of the Wee Folk, and people said there was fairy blood in his veins. His name was Peter MacBray, but everyone called him Brownie Pete, because he looked so much like a brownie, with his funny pointed beard and dancing black eyes, and his odd, shapeless hat that looked as if it had seen more winters than the mountains. Although Brownie Pete was bigger than a real brownie, he was still very small—hardly bigger than Martha. But he had the voice of a giant, a clear, ringing voice that could be heard all across the valley when he was up on the hills calling his sheep. It rang out now, calm and pleased and full of glee.

"I heard there was to be a christening today," he said, "and I says to meself, Pete old friend, where there's a christenin' there's a percession, and where there's a percession there's a bonny lass in front with jest enough bread and cheese to fill an old man's belly!" He made a low bow to Grisie and took off his hat with a flourish.

"I do be kerrect in thinkin' I'm the first man ye've encountered on the road, miss?"

Grisie stared at him, astonished, and then she smiled. Behind her Gavin Tervish burst out guffawing, and suddenly everyone was laughing. Brownie Pete had brought his sheep all the way down from the mountainside just to get a bit of bread and cheese. He was such a good shepherd that he would not leave his flock, but he thought nothing of herding them right through the middle of town and upsetting a whole christening party. Martha could see Mum laughing on the steps of the kirk, and even Father was smiling. The minister in his long robe tried to look sober, but his mouth quivered. Only Mrs. MacFarlane, the bairn's grandmother, did not smile. She glared at Brownie Pete. He didn't notice.

Grisie raised her chin. Even in the middle of the river of sheep she looked regal. She made a graceful curtsy to Brownie Pete and, without a word, reached into the basket and pulled out the napkin of bread and cheese. His eyes sparkled with pleasure.

"Hee hee! Cheese from the laird's larder! 'Tis a fine day for an old shepherd. A blessing on the bairn, and a blessing on the lass!" He bowed to Grisie, and tucked the napkin into a fold of his plaid. Then, without another word to the christening party, he raised his staff and waved it at the sheep.

"Hey la, ye sheep of mine! Get ye on yer way to the green hillside! Hey la, sheep, ye've grass to eat!"

The sheep surged forward along the lane that crossed the main road. They passed between the houses on the other side to the open land behind the village. Brownie Pete waved his staff at a few stragglers, and then, as suddenly as they had appeared, the strange old shepherd and his sheep were gone. The noise of their bleating grew softer and softer, until all Martha could hear were the occasional cries of "Hey la!" from Brownie Pete.

The people on the road and at the kirk door burst into loud talk. It was a christening procession that no one would ever forget. Mrs. Tervish and Grisie hurried toward the church, for the bairn had awakened again and was complaining about being stuck in the basket. Mum and Father moved forward to greet them. The minister waited at the top of the steps, smiling a welcome and looking relieved that the bairn had arrived without mishap. Mr. Tervish handed him a scrap of paper that had the baby's name written on it. The minister read the name silently, then smiled and nodded approvingly at Mr. Tervish. Martha couldn't wait to hear what name was on the paper.

"Bodes well for the bairn, it does," Martha heard Mrs. Sandy announce to a grim-faced Mrs. MacFarlane. "Brownie Pete is more than half fairy, or I'm a born fool. I'd no be surprised to hear he was a changeling, switched with the child of a good Christian woman at birth. If yer grandson has his blessin' and the minister's both, he'll grow up free o' care. Ye canna ask for better than to be favored by both sides!"

"Humph!" was all Mrs. MacFarlane said, but her angry forehead smoothed out a bit.

After all the excitement it was hard to settle down into a Sunday kind of mood. Martha sat on her bench next to Mum and tried not to fidget or swing her legs. She was very hungry and she feared the minister would hear her stomach growling from his pulpit. At last the long sermon and all the long prayers were over, and the minister dripped water on the bairn's forehead and announced that his name was Allan Alexander Tervish. Father smiled, pleased. The Tervishes had decided to name their son after him. Mum beamed at Mrs. Tervish. Then, just when Martha thought she would burst if she had to sit still one second longer, kirk was over and it was time to go outside for a celebration dinner on the grass.

A little way from the kirk was a wide field through which curved the stream. It was the town's bleaching-ground, where the women of the village laid out their linens to dry and whiten in the sun after washing them in the river. Today there were no drying linens; instead there were big tartan plaids spread out for people to sit on while they ate. Bowls and baskets of food were everywhere. Every household had brought something good to eat, in honor of the newly christened bairn.

Martha ate and ate and ate. There was sheep's-head broth and plum pottage, and stewed chicken and roast tripe, and cream sweetened with red-currant juice, and seed-cake and shortbread and pie. She was so full afterward that she could not have run around with the village children even if Mum had allowed her to.

The christening dinner lasted nearly three hours. Then it was time to file back into the kirk. Since kirk was only once a month, the minister must squeeze in as much preaching as he could fit into a day. It was even harder to settle down for the afternoon service. Martha and Duncan took turns pinching each other to keep from falling asleep. It seemed as if the final amen would never come.

By the time kirk was over, the sun was low in the sky. Martha leaned against Mum in the carriage and watched shadows reach across the stream. Out in the hills sheep were settling down for the night, and shepherds were spreading their plaids on the ground and sitting down for a bit of supper. Somewhere out there Brownie Pete was chuckling to himself over the good, rich cheese Cook had made and Grisie had carried. Martha thought about tiny

Allan Tervish, who hadn't had a name when he woke up this morning but had one now that would last him the rest of his life. She wondered who had carried Brownie Pete to the kirk when he was a bairn, and who had gotten the bread and cheese that day.

When the carriage drew up near Loch Caraid, the ferryman was waiting. The water made a lapping sound against the boat. The lake and the farm and the Stone House were a separate world from the village and the christening feast. The waves went on murmuring whether babes were named or not. The heather bloomed, and the grass grew, and the stones in the walls warmed in the sun and cooled in the dark. The lapping sound was like a lullaby, and Martha was asleep before the boat reached the other shore.

Fal al Diddle

One morning Mollie came in with the morning porridge earlier than usual. Not even Robbie was awake yet; the room was gray and still. The summer term had begun, and today the boys must go to school. They had to be out of the house before the sun rose, to make the long trip to the parish school in Clachan. They would be gone all day, every day but Sunday, until harvesttime.

Martha wished she could go with them. She would not mind getting up so early and eating her breakfast in the dark. It would be

exciting to cross the lake in the rowboat as
the sun came up. She would love to walk to
Clachan with her brothers and Sandy's children and Nannie's younger brothers and sisters. Duncan said they ran races and played
games the whole way to the village.

And Martha did not have to set foot in the
school to know she would like it there. Duncan
told her all about it as soon as he came home
each day. Duncan was so good at describing
things that Martha knew exactly what the
school looked like inside, and how the dominie
waved his arms around when he talked so that
the sleeves of his long black gown looked like
bat wings. The dominie was the teacher, and
Martha had seen him in church. But he did
not wear his black schoolmaster's gown to
church, only ordinary Sunday clothes.

She wished she could see the dominie's bat
wings with her own eyes. She would like to
sit at a desk beside Una Shaw or Annie Davis.
Martha was sure that if she went to school,
she would always know her lessons, and Mum
and Father would be very proud. And she

would learn more than just the reading and writing that the other little girls learned. She would listen to the boys' lessons and learn everything there was to know about history and arithmetic. She would learn to speak Latin, like Alisdair. Robbie was supposed to be learning Latin, too, but he hated it. Martha knew she would not hate it. She would remember every word the dominie said, and perhaps when she grew up she would go to college in Edinburgh. Alisdair was going to go, in a few years.

But Father said girls did not go to college. And the parish school, Father said, was not for the daughters of the laird. The tenants' daughters could go, but Martha must stay home with Grisie and Mum, and learn to sew and knit and spin. Mum was teaching her a bit of reading, too, and when Martha was a little older Mum would get her a governess to teach writing and arithmetic and needle-point. The governess Martha could barely remember, the one who had gotten married two springs ago, had taught Grisie how to read and write and do figures. Sometimes Mum made Grisie keep the household account books, for practice. She said arithmetic was very important for a lady to understand. Father took care of the estate, but it was Mum's job to keep track of every penny that was spent on food and clothing and household items. Mum said a laird's wife must be a wise manager, or she would find herself lady of a fine house full of hungry bellies.

Grisie did not like to study the accounts. She would rather sew or embroider. It was true that she had a fine hand with a needle—Father said the finest in the county. With a few bits of colored thread and a piece of good linen, Grisie could make a pillow covered with flowers that looked so real you could almost smell them, or little birds that seemed about to fly off the cloth. Before Grisie was thirteen years old, she had embroidered a whole border of fruits and leaves around one of Mum's best linen tablecloths. Father was so proud of it that he made Mum put it on the parlor table whenever guests came for dinner. The first time Martha had seen it she thought the tiny purple bilberries were real and had licked one, when she thought no one was looking. It tasted like thread and potato starch. Robbie had seen her and told the rest of the family. Father still liked to tell the story to visitors, and Martha only minded a little when everyone laughed at how silly she had been. After all, she had been a tiny wee girl then, just four years old. She would never make such a foolish mistake now.

But she did not think she would ever learn to embroider berries that looked good enough to eat, either. She hated to sew. The needle went into her fingers more times than it went into the cloth. Mum said it took a lot of practice to learn to make a good seam. Martha thought she would rather practice Latin, like Alisdair and Robbie. This year Duncan was going to begin studying Latin, too.

The days seemed long and dull with Duncan gone. There was no one to hide in the dairy with, or to play games with on the big rocky hill east of the lake. Grisie was busy with her sewing and embroidery much of the day, and Martha liked to be outside anyway.

Sometimes one of the farmers' wives let her help chase the milk cows out of the oat field. "Cushy, cushy, coo!" Martha would cry, just like the tenant women. "Get ye gone, noo!" And then the women would laugh to hear the laird's daughter sound just like a farmer's lass.

Some days Martha went to visit Mrs. Tervish in her cottage, to play with baby Allan. It was fun to make him laugh by tickling his toes one at a time as she chanted:

"This is the man that brak' the barn,
This is the man that stole the corn,
This is the man that stood and saw,
This is the man that ran awa,
And wee Peerie-Winkie paid for all!"

But she could hardly do that all day.

Mondays were the best days, for they were the Stone House's busy days. Mondays were the days the cowherd came down from the mountains.

Every summer most of Father's cattle were taken higher up into the mountains to live. The grass in the mountain glens was more plentiful than in the overgrazed meadows near the farm. Several men and women from the farm went up to the glens too, to look after the cattle. They lived in little huts that were thrown together quickly and hardly lasted through a summer. The cluster of huts was called a shieling, and the shieling was like a tiny village of its own that emptied out when winter came.

Each Monday a man came down from the shieling to pick up the week's supplies. Sometimes it was Nannie's brother Boggy, and sometimes it was Mr. Tervish's cousin Alf, and one hot day in late July it was a servant named Jacky. Martha had seen Jacky before, but she did not know him well. She watched as he led his horse slowly past the stables and the mains and brought it right up to the doorway of the Stone House. The horse was so loaded down with milk and butter and cheese that there was no room for Jacky. He had had to walk all the way from the shieling. Cook yelled for Mollie and Nannie. The butter must be weighed right away, and the milk and cheese had to be put into the cool dairy.

Jacky carried a crock of butter into the kitchen and put it down on the floor. Then he seemed to think he had done enough work, for he sank onto one of the hearth benches and leaned back with his hands folded on his stomach.

"Ahh," he sighed. "Noo all a man needs is a wee bit o' broth to tickle his belly." He eyed the big cauldron of soup bubbling over the fire.

Cook snorted. "A bit of broth, he says! Sure and ye well ken that broth is for the master's dinner. There be bannocks and cold porridge on the hearth—which ye may have *after* ye haul the rest o' that butter into me dairy!" Cook was always short-tempered on Monday. She hurried into the dairy to supervise the weighing of the butter. Mum kept records of how much milk and butter the cows produced each week.

"Miss Martha, lass! Run upstairs and tell yer mither the butter's here, that's a good girl!"

Martha raced upstairs and gave the message to Mum, who was going over the account books with Grisie. Grisie smiled with relief when Mum said Martha should tell Cook she'd be down straightaway.

"Might I work on my collar, then, while you're seeing to the servants, Mother?" Grisie asked. Martha did not stay to hear Mum's answer. She wheeled around and hurried back downstairs. It was exciting to watch the comings and goings on supply day.

When she came back into the kitchen, it was empty except for Jacky. He was on his way back from delivering the rest of the butter to Cook and Nannie in the dairy, and Martha watched him help himself to a bannock from the plate Cook had left on the hearth. With one eye watching the back door that led to the dairy, Jacky quietly dipped his bannock into the cauldron of broth.

Martha let out an indignant gasp. Jacky looked up in surprise, then grinned when he saw it was only Martha. He winked at her. Martha liked Sandy's winks but somehow she didn't like it when Jacky did it. It was as if he did not think her important enough to worry about. If Grisie had been the one to catch him dipping in the broth, he would have stammered an apology.

"Cook says a broth is hardly more than water until it has stewed for five hours," Martha said in her most grown-up voice.

"Och, aye, but 'tis water with chunks of meat floatin' aboot," Jacky replied, "and a bite of great-house mutton atop a good crisp bannock is a rare treat fer a man who's had naught but scrawny beef and lumpy porridge for three months gone!" He winked again and fished out another chunk of meat with his bannock.

In spite of herself Martha could hardly blame him. She would not like to eat the same thing morning, noon, and night for a whole summer. In a friendlier voice she said, "That's me mother coming down the stairs, you ken."

Then Jacky did look startled. He leaped away from the pot of broth and crammed the mutton into his mouth. He was wiping his chin with his hat when Mum entered the kitchen. Grisie came reluctantly after her. Mum must have said Grisie had to help with the supplies. Martha did not see why Grisie hated the task so much. She loved to help Mum count the items in the chests and closets, and choose just the right things to send up to the servants in the glens.

Cook came bustling back into the kitchen.

"A full stone's worth o' butter, ma'am!" she said to Mum. "Those cows earned their keep for once. And good sweet butter it is, too."

"That's fine, Cook," Mum said. "Please give my thanks to the women in the shieling," she told Jacky. He blushed and grinned, as if the compliment was meant for him instead of the women.

"The grass is uncommon good this year, my lady. Happen we'll stay an extra week or two, and I'm to tell ye the women will want more flax fer spinnin', for they've nearly finished what ye sent up last month. I've brought half the yarn down on me horse, if it please ye."

"Och, 'tis grand news, that!" Mum said. "And me just on the point of sending Sandy into the village to trade at the weaver's. That yarn will be just the thing for the boys' new shirts—if the quality is what it ought to be."

"I'm certain it is, your ladyship," Jacky mumbled nervously. Mum was known across the estate for being the kindest of mistresses, but her standards for linen and wool yarns were very high. Martha had often heard Mollie and Nannie whispering about how her lady-ship expected every servant to have as fine a hand with spinning as she herself did.

Nannie hated to spin. She said it was dreary work that made the fingers sting and the mouth dry. Martha thought it looked like much more fun than sewing. At least there were no needles on a spinning wheel and the wheel made a nice purring hum. But Nannie said she would rather mend socks or peel potatoes than spin. And yet Grisie and Mum and Mollie all loved spinning. Martha wondered why tasks that were fun for some people were like poison for others. Why would Duncan rather drink nasty-tasting tincture of rhubarb than help shear the sheep, and yet Robbie thought shearing was the greatest fun in the world? What made Alisdair love his studies so, when Robbie hated them? For that matter, Martha wanted to know, why weren't girls allowed to study the same things as boys? Why shouldn't she study Latin like Alisdair and Robbie? And she thought she would rather shear sheep than learn to sew. Sheep moved around, and you had to run and chase them out in the fresh air. But Mum said shearing was not for a laird's daughter.

Martha wondered who had decided what work belonged to which sort of person. If she were lady of an estate, she would let people do whatever interested them most.

Jacky had given Mum a list of the supplies the shieling-folk would need for the next week. A couple of extra blankets, for the nights were growing cool up in the high reaches. Three stone of meal, some salt, and a sack of potatoes if her ladyship could spare them. A new churn-dash, for one had been broken when a cow stepped on it. Mum said she could send him back right away with everything but the dash. Sandy could make a new one, but it would take time, and Jacky needed to leave soon if he was to make it to the shieling before dark.

"Canna one of you make one?" Mum asked.

Jacky shook his head. "There's scarce a branch of wood to be found, ma'am—naught stout enough to stand up to all that bumpin' and thumpin'. Happen I can get a good strong branch from his lairdship's wood afore I turn me way home?"

"Aye," Mum agreed. She told him to go find what he needed while she saw to the rest of the list. Then she sent Grisie to the attic for three bundles of flax to send to the spinners. Cook began measuring out the meal while Mum and Martha went to choose blankets from a chest in the nursery.

Before they had finished filling Jacky's list, three more men arrived. They were tenants from South Loch, one of Father's other farms. It was time for them to pay Father their labor dues. It was rare for a tenant farmer to have any coin money, and so he paid a part of his rent with labor. Four times a year the farmers came to cut wood for Father, or to cut squares of peat from the peat bog in the east of the valley. The rest of the rents were paid with a portion of the crops the farmers raised, and with other things like chickens and rabbits and pigeons.

Today the men from South Loch had come to cut wood. Mum sent them to the flax field to find Father. Jacky, his horse loaded with supplies, left just afterward to go back to the shieling. As he led the horse out of the yard he tossed a last wink back at Martha.

"Those farmers will be wanting supper tonight," Mum told Cook. "Best make up some extra bannocks and have Sandy bring a new cask of ale from the alehouse."

After supper that evening Mum told the children they might go down to the kitchen for a bit, to hear the singing. They must not stay long, for it was nearly bedtime and the boys had school the next morning. But even a few minutes was a treat when the kitchen was as full and merry as it was tonight. The men who had come to cut timber had been given their suppers in the kitchen. Then they lingered awhile to trade stories and songs with Cook and the maids and Sandy and Mrs. Sandy, who had come up to the Stone House for news from South Loch.

When the children appeared in the kitchen, there was a great chorus of greeting. John Grant, a South Loch farmer, struck up a lively tune on his fiddle. It was an air called "Tintock-Top." Martha clapped her hands. It was a favorite of hers. They all sang together:

> "On Tintock-Top there is a mist,
> And in the mist there is a chest,
> And in the chest there is a cup,
> And in the cup there is a drop;
> Tak' up the cup, drink off the drop,
> And set the cup on Tintock-Top!"

And then it all started over again, faster; and each time through, John Grant's bow moved faster and faster over the fiddle strings, until tongues tripped over the words and no one could sing for laughing.

Next John Grant played a slower tune while a farmer named Cuppy Briggs sang a long sad song about a mother whose sons were lost at sea, one by one. Cuppy's voice was quavery and high and almost sounded like crying. Martha liked it better when John Grant played lively tunes that made her feet tap. Cook sang a song about a merchant's son that Martha did not understand, but the grown-ups all thought it very funny. Everyone joined in on the chorus, shouting:

"Fal al diddle di do
Fal al da day!"

But all too soon, Cook said it was time for bairns to be in bed. The fiddle's voice grew soft and sweet, and Mollie's low, clear voice floated up the stairs behind the children:

"And hush-a-ba, birdie, croon, croon,
Hush-a-ba, birdie, croon;

The sheep are gane to the silver wood,
And the cows are gane to the broom, broom.

"And it's braw milkin' the kye, kye,
It's braw milkin' the kye,
The birds are singin', the bells are ringin',
The wild deer come gallopin' by, by."

Upstairs, tucked into the box bed beside Grisie, Martha could hear the soft music drifting up from below. She thought she would stay awake until all the singing was finished. But the next morning all she could remember was Mollie's faraway voice murmuring:

"And hush-a-ba, birdie, croon, croon,
Hush-a-ba, birdie, croon;
The goats are gane to the mountain high,
And they'll no be hame till noon, noon."

The Dust-gown

Suddenly it was August, and school was closed for the harvest. The farmers' children were needed in the fields. Even some of the village children came across the lake to help. Martha and Duncan often walked out to the flax field to see if Duncan's classmates Lewis and Ian were there. Lewis Tucker's father was the blacksmith in Clachan, and Ian Cameron's father was the village weaver, but the boys often came up to the farm to earn extra pennies for their families.

One morning when Martha and Duncan got

to the flax field, Mr. Tervish told them that none of the village children had come today. The ferryman had taken his family to visit their granny in Lochearnhead, and the villagers had no way to get across the lake.

Duncan decided to go out to the hay field instead, to watch the men swinging their scythes. Sometimes they let Duncan help, for Father had said that it would do his sons good to get some learning for their hands as well as their heads. But Martha was never allowed to get close to the sharp scythes. She could only stand to the side and watch.

"No, let's play Picts and Scots on the hill," she said to Duncan. Duncan shrugged and nodded his head.

The hill was called the Creag, which meant "pointed rock." It was not a mountain like the peaks that rose behind the Stone House. The Creag was only a very steep and rocky hill at the far end of Loch Caraid. But from the top Martha could see the whole shore of the lake, from the Stone House at the other end to the stream at the foot of the lake that flowed south into big Loch Earn.

The steep western slope of the Creag was more rock than grass. At the top the hill flattened out into a wide plateau, thick with heather, that slanted gently down to the moorland on the other side. Nobody lived on that wide grassy stretch of land except some shepherds and Auld Mary. If there was a mist, Auld Mary's hut could not be seen at all. Today Martha could just make out its squat brown shape, like a little lonely toadstool on the moor.

Along the crest of the hill ran a crumbling stone wall. Father said it had been built a thousand years ago, centuries before Edward MacNab had come to the valley. No one knew what it was supposed to have walled in, or kept out.

The bit of wall that was left was great fun to climb on. It was not very high, except for one tall corner post. By squeezing her fingers and toes into the spaces between stones, Martha could pull herself up to the very top.

"I'll be the Scots warrior this time," she said as she reached the top of the wall, panting with the effort of climbing.

"Aye," Duncan agreed, heading down the grassy side of the hill. He would play the Pict army, invading Martha's fortress. The Picts and Scots had been warring tribes who lived long, long ago, before Scotland was called Scotland. Alisdair liked to read Father's history books, and he had told Martha all about how the Scots had eventually conquered the Picts, and that was how Scotland got its name.

She and Duncan always played that the wall belonged to a Scottish chief, and his soldiers had to defend it against the wild Pictish army that raced up the hill shrieking terrible war-cries. Martha liked to be a Pict. Duncan said she had the best war-cry in the family. But it was fun to be a Scot, too, and crouch on top of the corner post pretending to pour a cauldron of boiling oil on the invaders.

Martha made it to the top of the post and looked all around. The tall grass of the hillside bent and dipped beneath the wind. She turned around to look at the Stone House. She could see the tops of the fruit trees in the kitchen garden, and the barns and the carriage-house a little way down the hill. She could see the farmers' cottages and Sandy's hut, and the hay fields and the oat fields and the green rows of turnips and potatoes beyond them. Below her Loch Caraid was a blue mirror reflecting the sky.

Then some movement on the Creag's rocky slope caught her eye.

"Robbie and Alisdair are coming," she called to Duncan.

Duncan frowned. Picts and Scots was a different game when Robbie played it. He was older and faster and stronger, so he always came out ahead in the battles.

"Wait for us!" Robbie yelled when he spotted Martha.

Duncan came back up the hill. Martha sighed. They would have to choose armies now. It would work out evenly if Alisdair would play, but he never did. He said he was too old for the running and screaming. Robbie always teased Alisdair that he was sober as a man of sixty. When Alisdair came to the hill, he spent most of his time digging around in the soil, looking for arrowheads or anything else that might have belonged to the ancient builders of the wall. He never found anything.

"Then we'll have to take turns, two against one," Duncan said. "I wish Ian or Lewis was here."

Martha told Duncan and Robbie they could side together first. It was harder to avoid mock arrows when you were running up the hill than when you were squatting on the post with your imaginary shield in front of you.

But Robbie only laughed. "Let a bit of a lass like you defend a post all on her own? What kind of coward do you take me for?" He shrugged at Duncan. "You can have her. I can handle the both of you." Still laughing, he ran to the bottom of the hill.

Martha stuck out her tongue at his back. *A bit of a lass! You can have her!* She exchanged a look with Duncan. They must win this battle.

She had an idea. Duncan took up a position next to Martha on the wall. Martha crouched

on the corner post as if she were ready with bow and arrow for the attack. With an ear-splitting whoop Robbie ran up the slope toward the wall. He held an imaginary shield above his head, knowing Martha would be changing her bow and arrow into a cauldron of oil. But Martha surprised him. With the wildest, loud-est battle cry she'd ever given, she leaped off the wall and landed right on top of Robbie.

She heard Robbie make a funny whoofing noise, as if she'd knocked the wind out of him, and then she was rolling down the hill and leaving her brother behind. She was going too fast to stop. The world went around her in a dizzy blur. At last she was slowing, and then she was lying in the grass at the bottom of the hill. She stared up at clouds wheeling around in the sky.

"Martha!" Duncan yelled. He ran to her side. "Are you hurt?"

"Nay, I think not," she said. She sat up slowly. "Just dizzy. Me knee smarts. I think I hit a rock."

Duncan helped her to her feet. He winced

at the sight of her dust-gown. It was streaked with dirt and grass stains, and there was a long ragged tear near the hem. Worst of all, she must have rolled over a fresh pile of cow dung. The farmers often led their cows out this way in the morning to graze on the moor grasses beyond the Creag.

Martha wrinkled her nose. She didn't smell very good.

Mum would not be pleased. It was very naughty to ruin clothes. Grisie would never have come home with a torn or stained gown, not even when she was a little girl like Martha. She always played quietly, like a lady. She would not jump off a wall onto a brother.

But Martha thought of Robbie's shocked face and decided she didn't care.

She followed Duncan back up the hill. Robbie was sitting dazed against the stone wall, glaring at Alisdair, who was doubled up with laughter.

"Dropped you like a rabbit, she did!" Alisdair crowed.

"I'll drop you if you don't watch out,"

Robbie said sourly. Then, catching sight of Martha's tousled hair and torn dress, he shook his head and gave a slow grin.

"Now, what kind of a lady jumps off walls onto poor unsuspecting soldiers?" he said.

The shadow of the Creag was just beginning to creep across the foot of the lake. It was one o'clock, time to go home for dinner. Martha and her brothers scrambled down the rocky path to the lakeshore.

The Stone House looked proud and lordly against the green hill and blue sky. The front door was flung wide open to let in air and sun. Next to the door was a bench made of mounded earth and covered with heather, where Mum could sit and watch the lake. The heather was in full purple bloom today, thicker and softer than any cushion.

But Martha had no eyes for the heather. Sandy was just leaving the yard, leading a horse toward the stable. The horse wore a fine saddle and its mane was brushed smooth. Martha hadn't known Mum and Father were expecting company.

She and Duncan exchanged nervous looks. Father would not like a guest to see his little girl looking so dirty.

"Ken you whose horse it is?" she asked.

"The duke of Argyle's," Robbie said. "Better practice your curtsy."

Martha's heart gave a sick thud, but Alisdair said, "He's only teasing, Martha. It isn't any duke. Dukes don't drop in unannounced, with only one horse and no servants. That horse belongs to Laird Alroch. Look at the crest on the saddle."

That was better, but still, Father and Mum were not going to be pleased. Alisdair picked some grass out of Martha's hair and wiped a smudge off her cheek. But he could only stare helplessly at her dust-gown.

"Are they in the parlor?" Martha whispered.

Duncan and Robbie crept into the house to peek and came back quickly.

"Aye," Duncan said. His eyes were worried. When dinner was in the parlor, it was a very special occasion.

"Leave your dust-gown in the kitchen,"

Alisdair suggested. "Your dress is all right, isn't it? You can explain to Mum later."

That was a good idea. Then she would not disgrace her mother and father by appearing before a guest in such a state. Martha pulled the filthy dust-gown off and wadded it up. She followed the boys inside. But before they reached the kitchen, Grisie called to them from the parlor doorway.

"Come on," she hissed. "Father's waiting. We have company."

"But we haven't washed up yet," Alisdair began.

"Then these two ought not to have stuck their big heads in the doorway!" Grisie retorted, nodding at Duncan and Robbie. "Saw you, Father did, and sent me to find out what's happened to your manners. Did you leave them on the hill?"

"We're coming," Robbie said. "Come on, Martha."

There was no hope for it. Martha would have to take the dust-gown into the parlor with her. She didn't know if it would be worse to put it back on, or to carry it into the parlor where dirty laundry did not belong. At least Grisie hadn't noticed yet. She would scold worse than Mum. Holding the gown behind her back, Martha slowly trailed after Grisie and the boys into the parlor.

The parlor was a large, solemn room that was used only for company and holidays. In the middle of the room was the enormous, polished wooden table that Father's grand-father had brought from England. It could seat twelve people. A pair of silver candlesticks stood in the center upon Grisie's embroidered cloth.

There was a tall case of books in the cor-ner, next to a little one-legged table upon which rested the enormous family Bible. The parlor also had a sideboard and a china closet made of real mahogany. Father's father had had them specially made in Edinburgh. The rich red-brown wood was smooth as satin. But Father said the money would have been better spent on the land. He did not hold with spending money on fine furnishings, when there was so much to be done on the estate.

Against the staircase wall was an old box bed that had been in Mum's family for a hundred years. It was for guests to sleep in, when they stayed overnight. Mum said Uncle Harry's family would come to visit this winter. Uncle Harry and Aunt Grisell would sleep in the parlor. The cousins would sleep in the nursery with Martha and Grisie and the boys. But Martha was not thinking about winter now.

Laird Alroch was standing at the hearth beside Father. He was a nice old man who lived in a stone castle on the other side of the mountain. Father said he owned all the land from Meall na Cloiche to Lochearnhead. He was a very important man, who had had a seat in Parliament in Edinburgh before he got too old to make the journey more than once a year. But he was not frightening and solemn like other great lairds Martha had heard of. Laird Alroch had kind, twinkling eyes and a pocket that was always filled with sugar candies for small children. He had not been

angry the time that Martha had asked him if
he was bald. He had chuckled for a long time,
and then he took off his curled gray wig and
let her feel his smooth round head. It had not
felt like an egg after all, but it was just as
smooth.

But that had been years ago, when Martha
was hardly more than a baby. Now she was
older and she ought to be better behaved.
Martha's cheeks burned with shame. She did
not want to disgrace herself in front of Laird
Alroch.

Suddenly she realized that no one was looking at her. The boys were in front of Martha.
There was a commotion of hugging and my-
how-you've-growns, for Laird Alroch had not
been across the mountain for a visit in half
a year. No one had noticed Martha hanging
toward the back with her crumpled dust-gown
in her hands. She looked around wildly. The
door of the box bed was open. Quickly, without stopping to think or breathe, she stuffed
the dust-gown under the pillow.

Her heart pounding, she whirled around. No

one had seen her. It had taken only a second. She was lucky the bed had been open. Usually it was kept closed.

Then everyone was staring at her, and Laird Alroch was wondering loudly where his hug was. Martha crossed to the hearth and kissed his wrinkled cheek. Inside she was trembling. Suppose Mum asked why she wasn't wearing her dust-gown? She would have to tell everyone how naughty she had been. But no one asked. She saw her brothers looking at her with curious glances, but she could not tell them anything. Laird Alroch tapped his breast pocket, where he always kept the candies, and winked at Martha.

"Ye can take a peek noo, but we must leave them till after dinner or your good mither will have me hide!" he said.

"And speaking of dinner, here it is at last," said Mum. Mollie came into the parlor with a huge tureen of sheep's-head broth. She placed it on the table near Father's chair. Nannie came just behind her with a platter of potatoes and turnips.

"Tatties and neeps!" Laird Alroch beamed. "Me favorite!"

They all sat down and Father said the blessing. Then Mum filled Martha's bowl with the good, rich broth full of barley and vegetables. Martha ate every drop, and two slices of chicken, and a plate of tatties and neeps and two bannocks and a large wedge of cheese. She was almost too full for the pudding when Mollie brought it out. But there were plums in it, because Laird Alroch was here, and Martha ate a whole dishful.

Laird Alroch told a story about the terrible week last spring when his cook had gone to tend her sick mother, and his housemaid had gotten married and moved away, and all three of his kitchenmaids fell ill at once. He had called in two women from the village near his castle to help with the cooking, but he had not known that one of them had stolen the other one's sweetheart seventeen years before. They had carried the fight through all the long years since—even though the stolen beau had turned out to be no prize, and both women had been happily married to two entirely different men for fifteen years. The feuding women had turned Laird Alroch's kitchen upside-down with their quarrels. They had broken three of his fine china plates and one large earthenware jug that his great-grandmother had owned. They were so distracted with fighting that they burned the porridge and salted the berries and served him a dish of singed sheep's-head—Laird Alroch's favorite, when it was properly cooked—with the wool only half singed off.

"So much wool did I swallow that day, ye could have turned me inside-out an' used me as a blanket!"

Mum's merry laugh rang above Father's booming one. Laird Alroch's eyes twinkled.

"I tell ye, Margaret, me dear," he went on, "ye nivver saw a happier man than I was when me own fine cook came home the next week. Thought I'd gone out of my head, she did, when I told her her porridge was finer than manna from heaven." He took a bite of his pudding, and sighed with pleasure. "But not even her pudding could rival this one. Ye've a treasure in that cook of yours, Margaret."

The pudding was so good and Laird Alroch's story was so funny that Martha forgot all about the dust-gown.

She did not remember it when Father said he was glad Laird Alroch was staying the night, for he wanted to show him the larch plantation and the west turnip field that afternoon. She did not think of it once all the long afternoon, for Cook was making a chestnut pie and she let Martha help her take the stones out of the raisins and roll out the crust. Then Mum set Martha to work at her sewing sampler, and Martha had no thought for anything but the number of pricks she gave her finger with the needle.

Soon it was suppertime. Cook had made a good supper of cabbage and potatoes and savory roasted rabbit. Dinner was the big meal of the day, and supper was usually just broth and oatcakes, and perhaps some good rich whey to drink if there was any left from Cook's cheese making. But tonight there were extra dishes for supper in honor of Laird Alroch.

After the dishes had been cleared, Father went to the fire and put another peat on the flames. He pulled chairs near the hearth for Mum, Laird Alroch, and himself. Martha, Grisie, and the boys gathered close on the hearth benches. The big ale cups were brought out, and a jug of ale that Sandy had brewed last winter. And Cook had saved some whey for the children.

Martha held Lady Flora in her lap and drank the whey, the part of the milk that got squeezed out when the milk was turned into curds for cheese making. It was cool and delicious. She listened to Father and Laird Alroch talk. Mum's fingers flashed back and forth above her knitting needles, as quick and light as her laugh. Laird Alroch sang a funny song about a traveling fish-seller. Martha wondered who he told his jokes to when he was at his home. No one lived there with him but the servants. His wife had died many years ago, and all three of his sons had been killed in the battle at Culloden during the Rising of

1745. It did not seem fair that Laird Alroch should have been left alone. Martha wished he could live with her family in the Stone House. Then he could make Father laugh with his stories every night, and he could teach Martha and Duncan all the songs he knew. Mum said no one living knew more songs than Laird Alroch, except perhaps Auld Mary.

The reedy voice singing and the good whey filling her belly made Martha very sleepy. She was almost too tired to wait for Mum to say "Get into your nightclothes." She thought she might like to curl up right there, beside the fire, like a cat. Lady Flora felt heavy in her arms. At last Mum said it was bedtime. Martha held Grisie's hand as they went to the nursery, with the sound of Laird Alroch's ballad rising up the stairs behind them.

It was not until Martha climbed into bed that she remembered the dust-gown. As she snuggled in next to Grisie and lay her head on the pillow, another pillow flashed into her mind—a fat feather pillow in a crisp linen pillowcase, with something dirty and torn wadded up beneath it. The dust-gown was still in the box bed!

And Laird Alroch was sleeping there.

Martha cried out in dismay. She was wide awake now. Grisie rolled over and stared at her.

"What is it?" she asked. "Be you sick?"

"Nay," Martha groaned. She almost wished she were sick. She wished a terrible fever would strike her, and then Mum and Father would be so worried, they would not mind at all about the dust-gown.

But though her cheeks felt flaming hot, she knew she had no fever. She did not see how she could have been so foolish. Why else would the box bed have been open, unless it were being aired out for a guest to sleep in? Why else would it have been made up with freshly bleached sheets and a fine, fat pillow? Pillows could not be left in the bed when no one was visiting, for mice would be sure to get in and nest in the feathers.

"Martha! Tell me what ails you!" Grisie said. She sat up in bed, her eyes wide and worried. "Should I call Mother?"

"Nay, nay," Martha said quickly. "I'm not sick. I just remembered something, that's all."

Grisie snorted. "Ah, come to bed without washing behind the ears again, did you? Well, you'd best start remembering. I'll not be having all the dirt of the moor rub off your neck onto my pillow, do you hear me?"

Martha started to protest, then remembered that Grisie was right. She *had* forgotten to wash behind her ears.

"Aye," she muttered, rolling over on her side.

"We all hear you!" came Alisdair's muffled voice from across the room. "Stop your squawking, will you? Some of us are trying to sleep in this room."

Martha wanted to sleep, but she could not. She thought about kind Laird Alroch finding her dirty dust-gown in his bed. Or perhaps he would not find it, but would lie in the closed box bed all night wondering where the smell of cow dung was coming from.

She had disgraced Mum worse than if she had come to dinner wearing the dust-gown.

144

Tomorrow the whole family and all the servants, too, would know how Martha had shamed her family. The laird's daughter! Grisie would never have done such a naughty thing.

Martha did not know when she fell asleep. She only knew that the night seemed very long.

Laird Alroch was to leave just after breakfast. He had a long ride ahead of him. Mum had said it was very difficult for him to make such a trip, for his hands were crippled with rheumatism, and it was painful for him to hold the horse's reins.

Cook had made a big breakfast of yeast buns and salt cod. Mollie came into the nursery and said the children were wanted in the parlor. It was a special treat to eat breakfast in the parlor, with Father and Mum and Laird Alroch. But Martha could not feel excited. She moved very slowly pulling her petticoat and dress over her head.

"Come on, Martha!" Grisie said impatiently. "Unless you want to button yourself. We mustn't be late for a parlor breakfast!"

It could not be helped. Martha must put on her clothes and go downstairs. She wondered if Laird Alroch had already told Mum and Father, or if he would wait until Martha was there.

Father did not look stern, so he did not know yet. Martha walked slowly to the table. She could not look at Laird Alroch. She waited for him to speak.

But he only wished a good morning to Grisie and then to Martha. Everyone sat down and Mollie came behind their chairs to dish out the porridge. Alisdair asked Laird Alroch a lot of questions about Glasgow. Laird Alroch's voice was not at all cross when he answered.

At last Martha dared to look at him. The old man was watching her. His eyes twinkled at her. Very slowly, he winked.

Martha forgot she had a bite of fish in her mouth and tried to put in another. She coughed a little, and Mum scolded her for stuffing herself. But there was no anger or disappointment in her eyes when she looked at Martha.

Martha began to wonder if perhaps Laird Alroch was not going to tell on her after all.

As soon as breakfast was over, Laird Alroch began to say his good-byes. He would not be back for many months, perhaps not before winter.

"Me old bones need a bit o' rest," he said. But he promised to come for a visit at the New Year.

At the very last, he stooped down to speak to Martha. "I have a boon to ask of ye, bonnie lassie," he said. "I've a bag of sweeties here that's weighing me doon. 'Tis glad I'd be if ye'd take it off me hands and lighten my load!"

Martha took the bag and then put her arms around his neck. She hugged him, hard. He whispered something in her ear.

"If I were ye, I'd have a look underneath yer mither's china cabinet this mornin'. It looks as though the Wee Folk ha' been makin' mischief hereabouts, usin' yer clothes for their picnic blankets!" He winked at her again and then slowly straightened up. He climbed upon the loupin'-on stone to mount his horse.

Martha saw him wince a little when he took the reins, as if it hurt his hands to hold them in that position. That must be the rheumatism. Martha felt sorry that such a nice man should suffer any pain. He had not told on her about the dust-gown. He had helped her by hiding it where she could sneak it away without anyone finding out. Martha felt a strange lump in her throat. She stood still, watching him ride slowly down the path toward the mountains. Duncan and Robbie ran beside his horse for a little while. Martha wanted to run, too, but she could not move. She knew she must go in and get her dust-gown out of its hiding place before Mollie went into the parlor to do her sweeping.

"Martha!" Mum said. Martha jumped. Laird Alroch had ridden out of sight. Mum was looking at Martha curiously.

"Is something amiss?" she asked. "You're staring at naught!"

"No!" Martha said. "I mean—I mean—aye." She looked at the ground. Father had gone into the house. Mum stood quietly, waiting.

Martha swallowed down the lump in her throat. In a very small voice she told Mum the whole story—about ruining the dust-gown, and hiding it in the bed, and Laird Alroch keeping her secret to save her from disgrace.

Mum's face was grave. The smile that never left her eyes was buried very deep. But it was still there, a little. Martha did not feel quite as bad as she had felt all night.

"I think you know how naughty you have been," Mum said. "You should not have tried to hide your dust-gown. That was deceitful, which is a kind of lying."

"Lying!" Martha's eyes opened wide. "But I didna tell any lies—"

"Nay, not with words. But by pretending that naught was wrong, when you knew it was, you were telling a lie just as surely as if you'd spoken it."

The lump was back, bigger now.

But Mum said, "I'll not go on about it. You understand it now, do you not?"

Silently Martha nodded.

"Then the matter 'tis finished. Laird Alroch is a kind man. Not many would take such trouble to keep a small lass from a scolding she well deserves!" Mum put her hand on Martha's head. "Come. Let's see if a good soaking will take the stains out of that dust-gown. If it's that much spirit you have that you must go jumping off walls and rolling down hills, you can certainly manage to do a little scrubbing in the laundry tub!"

"Truly?" Martha asked. She had always wanted to help the maids with the washing, but they always said she must not get her frock wet. Now, at last, Mum was going to let her try it out!

It did not seem right, somehow, that she should get to do something fun after she'd been so naughty. But she would still have to sew up the tear. That would be punishment, for certain.

She went into the house with Mum, thinking about kind Laird Alroch. He had been nicer to her than she deserved. She wished she could do something for the old laird, to thank him. She made up her mind. She'd think of something, even if it meant pricking her fingers to bits to sew him a cravat to wear around his neck.

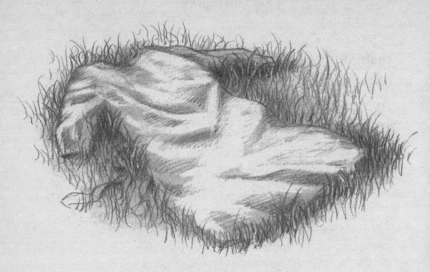

Washing-Day

In fair weather washing-day came once a week. Martha was glad the days were still warm, for if winter's chill had set in already, she might have had to wait a month or more to help with the washing. In the winter the wash water had to be heated on a peat fire, and it took a great deal of peat to heat enough water.

Peat must never be wasted, and so washing could not be done too often when the weather was cold. But in summer there was no need to heat water for washing. The cool, clean lake water was fine just as it was. Mollie said she looked forward to summer's weekly washing-days, for it gave her a chance to cool her feet.

This week Martha looked forward to it too. When washing-day came, she could hardly wait for the morning chores to be over so that the washing would begin. But Mum made her work on her sewing sampler first. The minutes seemed like hours as she struggled to make the needle go where it was supposed to. She knew that as soon as her dust-gown was clean and dry, she would have to begin sewing up the tear in the hem. But she was glad when at last Mum said it was time for her to go down to the lake.

It was a dazzlingly blue day. The sky and the lake were each so blue that it seemed as if one was trying to outdo the other. They cast their blueness onto the hills along with the golden sun, so that the hills were a soft deep green with blue shadows in the hollows and brilliant patches of light on the crests. Clover bloomed on the hillside, and fat honeybees buzzed among the round pink flowers.

Nannie and Mollie had already hauled the big washtub down to the lochside. Mollie had gone back to the house for the soap, while Nannie began to fill the washtub with water from the lake. A rush basket filled with clothes lay beside her on the grass. Martha's dust-gown was still soaking in a pail of water. Martha felt a little guilty prickle in her stomach when she saw it but the sun was so warm and the water looked so inviting it was easy to forget what she had done that brought her here.

Soon Mollie came hurrying back with the soap that she and Mum and Cook had made from tallow and oak ashes.

"Well!" she said, shaking her head at the heaping clothes basket. "'Tis a good thing we have a helper this day, such a mountain of laundry do we have!"

"I was just thinkin' the same thing meself," said Nannie.

Mollie tucked her skirt up above her knees, pushing the hem well down into her apron so that the skirt would not get wet. Her legs and feet were bare. Then she dunked a pile of clothing into the tub of water, stirring with her arms so that all the clothes were soaked through. Next she took the soap and rubbed it over the clothes to work up a lather.

When the clothes were well soaped, she climbed right into the tub on top of them. The frothy water came almost to her knees. She began to stomp, up and down, up and down, working the dirt out of the clothes with her feet.

"Shall we gie her a hand, Miss Martha?" Nannie smiled. She began to sing. It was a loud, hearty song and Mollie stomped in time to the music. Nannie did not have Mollie's sweet, pure voice, but she sang with spirit, her eyes snapping with fun. Martha sang too. They must help Mollie keep up a good vigorous rhythm of stamping.

> "'Twas in the month o' sweet July
> Just as the sun shone in the sky
> It was in atween the rigs o' rye
> Sure I heard twa lovers talkin'—"

Martha knew the song well, for Cook often sang it as she chopped vegetables. It was about a young man and his sweetheart, who went out to the rye field to have a talk. The young man told the girl he must go away to seek his fortune. He did not want to leave her but thought it was best.

Martha and Nannie sang:

"Your father takes o' you great care
Your mither combs your yellow hair
But your sisters say that ye'll get nae share
If ye follow wi' me, a stranger."

In the end the lass decided to go away with her sweetheart, though her father might fret and her mother might frown. The girl got no share of her inheritance, and she never saw her parents or her sisters again. It hardly seemed possible that anyone could go so far from home that she could never get back. Martha could not imagine leaving Mum and Father and never seeing Glencaraid again. She knew Mollie lived far away from her family; she had come from

Loch Katrine, many miles to the southwest, and had not been home once in the two years since she had come to work in the Stone House. Martha thought she would like to go over the mountains to see Loch Katrine—Mollie said it was just as beautiful as Loch Caraid, but Martha wanted to see for herself and make up her own mind. She only wanted to visit, though. She would not like to live anywhere but in her own valley.

Martha didn't like to think of the mother and father in the song missing their lass, but she liked the last verses, and she sang them with gusto as Mollie tramped in the tub.

> *"This lad he was a gallant bold,*
> *A brave fellow just nineteen years old.*
> *He's made the hills an' the valleys roar*
> *An' the bonnie lassie she's gane wi' him.*

> *"This couple they are married noo*
> *An' they've got bairnies one or two*
> *They bide in Brechin the winter through*
> *And in Montrose in the summer!"*

157

Martha liked the part about the lad making the hills and valleys roar. She wondered how he had done it. Did he have some fairy-magic, that could make the hills open mouths and call out? Or perhaps the lad himself could whoop so loud that he brought out the echoes that hid in the corners of the valley. Duncan's friend Lewis could do that. When he played Picts and Scots, you could hear his war-cry all the way back at the Stone House. It was funny, because usually he was a very quiet person. Lewis said he heard enough noise at his father's blacksmith shop, what with the banging of the iron and the roaring of the fire. When he was outside, he liked to be still and listen to the soft sounds of the lake and the wind—except, of course, when he was called upon to lead a Pictish army to battle.

Mollie's mouth was drawn into a thin line of concentration. The water splashed around her knees, and her legs flashed in and out of the splashes. Sometimes a piece of clothing bobbed to the top of the tub in a swirl of bubbles. There were Duncan's dark green breeches; there was one of Father's tartan socks. A blue plaid dress floated up and was stomped back down. Martha knew it must be Grisie's, for she was wearing her own blue plaid.

Mum had sewn most of these clothes with her own hands. All the linen and wool yarn that Mum and Grisie and the maids spun went to the weaver in Clachan to be turned into cloth. Sandy would ride to Clachan and come back with great rolls of cloth for Mum to cut and sew. But before the yarn was woven, it must be dyed, and that was when Auld Mary came to visit. She knew all there was to know about what plants to boil to make colors leak out into the water. When yarn was soaked in the water, it came out yellow or red or green or brown, just as Auld Mary said. It seemed like magic to Martha, but Auld Mary said plant dyes were one thing the fairies could not take credit for—they were one of the good Lord's gifts to mortals, just like cool water on a hot day and peat fire in the cold.

Mum said dyes were one of His sweetest

gifts, for color meant more to a Highlander than to anyone else in the world. Without the special dyes that came from the moor plants, the weaver could not make tartans. A tartan plaid must have stripes of many different colors, crossing and crisscrossing each other. Martha spotted another one of Father's socks in the water, with its cheerful green and red squares. She was glad Mum and Auld Mary knew about dyes, so that Father could be a proper Highlander.

"Miss Martha!" Mollie called briskly, panting from all her stomping up and down. "Ye'll want to do a bit o' scrubbin' on yer liddle dustgown before we throw it in the tub. Them stains need a careful hand if they're to come out!"

"Aye, and no a careless foot!" Nannie laughed, ducking as a great wave of water splashed out from the tub and sprinkled the clothes she was sorting on the grass. The colored linens and cottons were in the tub now, and then would come the whites, the aprons and nightgowns and sheets. At the last would come the woolen clothes, which must not be stomped so hard.

"Ye can tread on the woolens, miss," Nannie told Martha. "Yer wee feet will be just the thing to gentle the dirt out."

"Where's me song?" Mollie demanded. Nannie and Martha took up the tune again, while Nannie continued to sort, and Martha spread her dust-gown on a flat stone. She rubbed soap on the stains, wrinkling her nose at the soap's strong smell. She decided she would rather watch Mollie jumping up and down in the tub. Scrubbing with hands was hard work.

When Mollie was out of breath, she climbed out of the tub and changed the dirty water for fresh clean water from the lake. She rinsed the clothes well, shaking them out with her hands. She did not need to stomp for this part, for her feet had already worked out all the dirt. Nannie helped her wring the wet clothes. Then it was Nannie's turn to stomp on the whites.

Now Martha and Mollie sang for Nannie

while they spread the clean clothes out on the grass to dry. Martha's dust-gown was in the tub now, churning around with the linens under Nannie's feet.

When she had work to do, Mollie was brisk and busy, her eyes and hands fixed on her task, and her lovely voice rising above them. But when all the clothes were spread out, Mollie became playful. She clapped in time to the stomping, and then she winked at Martha and began to sing and clap a little faster. Martha clapped and sang, too, trying not to laugh. It was such fun to see Nannie gasping to keep up. Faster and faster they sang until Nannie's arms and legs were moving so quickly Martha could hardly see them through the splashing water. Nannie's face was red and her blond hair was coming loose. Her skirt was wet, too, even though she had tucked it up carefully.

At last Nannie was stomping so fast, she could hardly breathe—partly because she was laughing so hard. She climbed out of the tub and wrung water out of her skirt.

"The laugh's on you, Mollie Ferguson, for ye'll have to lend me yer extra frock," she said, grinning. "I've only the one, besides me Sunday dress. I canna serve dinner like this!"

"Och, this sun'll have ye dry in the blink o' an eye," said Mollie. "But the frock is yers to borrow if ye want it."

"Is it my turn now?" Martha asked.

Mollie and Nannie laughed. "Aye, 'tis nearly that," said Mollie. "As soon as ever we rinse these things in the new water."

Martha helped squeeze the water out of Father's linen shirts and Mum's good napkins, which had been used during Laird Alroch's visit. At last the woolen clothes were soaped and put into the tub. There was not as much water this time, for there were only a few woolens to wash, since the weather was still warm. Mollie helped tuck up Martha's skirt so it would not get wet.

Just as she had seen Mollie and Nannie do, Martha jumped up and down on the clothes. The cool water felt lovely on her bare feet and legs. Her hair bounced up and down and made her neck itch, but nothing could spoil the fun of stomping. Mollie and Nannie sang and clapped. Martha tried to sing too, but she soon understood why the person in the tub needed someone else to do the singing for her. It took too much breath to sing and stomp at once.

She looked down at her feet and watched the waves and foamy splashes. She saw the bright colors of the tartans churning in the water. She looked straight ahead and saw Mollie and Nannie bobbing up and down on the green grass. Only it wasn't really Mollie and Nannie doing the bobbing, it was she herself. She laughed to see the grassy shore and the outspread clothes and the smiling girls rippling up and down as if the whole world were floating on a giant raft in a giant lake. Water splashed up into her mouth. It tasted soapy.

"Och, mind the wool!" Mollie cried. "Who'd ha' thought such a tiny wee thing could stomp so hard!"

Martha stomped a little slower. It felt good

to slow down, and soon she stopped. She felt the way she felt after a race with Duncan, only wetter. Her toes were pink and wrinkled. When she climbed out of the tub, they stuck to the grass.

Most of the grass along the lakeshore was hidden by the drying clothes. After the woolens had been spread out, Mollie and Nannie went back to the house to get on with their chores. They left Martha to watch the clothes. She must make sure none of them blew into the lake.

Sitting there on the bank, her damp skirt drying, Martha watched a boat creep into view around a curve of the shoreline. Someone was fishing. Further down the shore she could see someone stooping at the edge of the water. It was Annie Davis. Mrs. Sandy must have sent her to fill a pail of water. Annie waved at Martha, and Martha waved back. She wanted to run and say hello to Annie but the wind had begun to puff a little harder and she could not leave the drying clothes.

Her dust-gown was spread on a gorse bush.

Whenever the wind gusted, its hem fluttered up and then sighed back down. The rip in the hem made a little window against the sky. Laird Alroch had said that it looked as though the Wee Folk had used the dust-gown for a picnic blanket. Martha wished that was true, so that maybe the fairies would come back and sew up the tear. They could use spider-silk for thread and then it would be a magic dust-gown, and when Martha put it on, per-haps she would be able to see the fairies.

Martha found a dandelion to wish on, but though she closed her eyes and wished with all her might, no fairies came to mend the rip. She kept her eyes closed so long that a nap-kin blew to the very edge of the water before she noticed it. After that she wished with her eyes open. Maybe the fairies would come at night, instead.

But the next morning the clean, dry dust-gown lay in the top of Mum's sewing basket, and the window in the hem was still wide open. Mum made Martha sit down beside her and begin to close it, stitch by stitch by stitch.

Auld Mary

By the time the hem was stitched up, many days later, Martha had decided she could not sew Laird Alroch a cravat after all. She hated the look of the mended tear, a puckered scar at the edge of her dust-gown. Grisie said Martha had done a good job for such a wee thing. Then Grisie glanced down at the smooth invisible seam of her own dress, which she had made herself. Martha hated her mended dust-gown all the more and felt disgusted with the whole general world of needles.

She wished she could learn to spin instead, but Mum said she was not big enough.

"You'll need a few inches yet before your foot can reach the treadle, me love." Mum smiled and her eyes took on a faraway look. "When I was a lass me auld auntie had a tiny wee spinning wheel just the right size for me. I was aye just your age when she taught me to use it. You'd have loved it, Martha." She sighed. "I wonder whatever became of it. Sold or burned when the family lost the house and moved to my uncle's estate in Skye, most like. 'Tis a pity we haven't a wheel like that now, but there it is. Never mind. You've plenty of other things to learn and plenty of years to learn them in."

But once Martha had thought of learning to spin she could not stop thinking of it. Every morning Mum put her to work on her sewing. Martha sat beside her sister and struggled to make the stitches march along a straight road, as Grisie's did. Somehow Martha's always looked more like a winding mountain path. Grisie did everything better.

Auld Mary

It was not fair being the youngest. Everyone could do things that Martha couldn't. Martha could knit a little, but she knew only two kinds of stitches, while Grisie knew dozens. Alisdair could read Latin and he knew all about history and politics. He could write in a hand as elegant as Father's, and also he had a plot of trees in the fir plantation that he had raised himself. Father said there was not a man on the estate who could outrun Robbie in a race. Duncan could carve whistles out of wood and he could draw birds and animals that looked almost real. And Grisie could sew and draw and read and write and do figures, and she could spin.

But Grisie had not learned to spin until she was eight. It occurred to Martha that if she could not do something *best*, perhaps she could do it *youngest*. After supper that night she watched closely as Mum sat at the spinning wheel. It was easy to see how spinning worked. Hadn't she watched Mum spin a thousand times already? There was hardly a night in the year when Mum's wheel was not humming.

The next day Mum and Grisie were out of the house all afternoon on a visit. Martha went up to the bedroom to look at the spinning wheel. It was made of smooth, cherry-brown wood and sat on three long carved legs. The wheel part was on one side, with a wooden rod connecting it to a pedal at the bottom. That was the treadle, which Mum stepped on to make the wheel revolve.

On the other side were three carved round sticks that pointed toward the ceiling. The two small ones side by side were the maidens, and they held between them a bobbin of spun yarn. The tall pole at the end was the distaff. It held a cone-shaped bundle of flax that had been soaked to separate the fibers, and then dried, beaten, and combed. The long, combed fibers were wrapped around the distaff.

Martha raised her fingers to touch the fuzzy loose end of the flax bundle. When spun, flax became a smooth, hard yarn called linen. The spinner pulled the hairs at the bottom of the flax bundle out into an airy web that narrowed until all the separate strands were twisted together by the spinning of the wheel into one fine thread.

The thread went through a little hole in one of the maidens and wrapped around the bobbin. The far end of the bobbin had a wide rim, around which was a kind of belt that was also wrapped around the edge of the big wheel. When the wheel turned, the belt moved and made the bobbin spin.

Martha could picture exactly how Mum sat in front of the wheel, pushing the treadle with her foot and holding one hand up to the bundle of flax. As the wheel turned, Mum's fingers kept drawing out strands of flax from the distaff and pinching them together so that they became one long continuous thread. The motion of the wheel caused the thread to wind itself around the bobbin. When Mum spun, it was like a kind of sitting-down dance. The wheel turned and the bobbin turned and the bundle of loose fibers was twisted into a strong, smooth thread. It was almost like magic.

Martha thought she would try it herself. She

sat on the stool but saw that Mum was right; her foot could not reach the treadle. So she tried standing up. She drew out several fibers from the bundle on the distaff, as she had seen Mum do. Then, pinching the fibers between her fingers, she stepped on the treadle.

The wheel spun quickly round. The bobbin turned and pulled the flax through her fingers. It burned a little. Martha let go in surprise. Then she remembered that Mum always dipped her fingers in a cup of water as she spun. She said flax must be spun damp, or it would be too brittle.

Martha licked her fingers the way she had seen Nannie and Mollie do and took hold of the drawn-out flax fibers once more. She stepped on the treadle. Again the spinning bobbin pulled the thread through her fingers. She held on and watched the thread wrap itself around the bobbin. She smiled to herself. She was spinning!

But the wheel was pulling the thread too quickly. She could not hold the fibers tight enough, and the thread that wrapped around the bobbin was thick and full of fuzzy slubs. It was almost too thick to fit through the hole in the maiden. Martha's hand could not draw out the new fibers from the bundle quick enough. Her thread did not look at all like Mum's. It hardly looked like thread at all. It was just a thick, fuzzy string.

She put out a hand to stop the wheel. Then she tried to spin again. It was very hard to keep the treadle going and hold the thread at the same time. Her arms and legs felt stretched out in too many directions. And it was hard to pull out just a few fibers from the bundle without pulling them so far that they came loose. She could not imagine how Mum— and Grisie—could keep hands and feet doing different things for so long without ever breaking the rhythm.

Perhaps it was much easier sitting down. If only her legs were longer. Mum had been right.

Mum would come and see that Martha had tried to spin. She would not be able to use the thread that Martha had made. It was too lumpy and bumpy, not at all fit for weaving or knitting. And Grisie would smile and say that it was not a bad job for a wee thing like Martha. It was not fair.

If only there were a way to make her legs longer. Everyone said she was growing like a weed, but the weeds in the garden got taller every day unless they were pulled out. Martha did not feel any taller today than she had been yesterday. People grew so slowly.

Cook always said that good, halesome food made people grow strong. Perhaps that was what made them grow tall, too. Martha wondered if perhaps there was a special food she could eat that would make her legs grow. She started to the kitchen to ask Cook, then thought better of it. Cook would tease her, and she'd probably tell Mum and Grisie all about it. There must be someone else Martha could ask. Mrs. Sandy? No—she'd tell Sandy and Sandy would tell Cook. Then Martha thought of someone better.

She would go see Auld Mary.

Auld Mary knew all there was to know about everything that grew. Whenever someone in the valley was sick, Auld Mary was sent for to heal him. She knew which herbs would cure sore throats, and chilblains, and toothache, and every kind of sickness. Perhaps she knew of an herb that made small girls grow more quickly, too. Some people even said Auld Mary was a witch. Surely a witch could help Martha to grow.

Martha set off at once. She cut across the heathery grass behind the farmers' cottages and ran all the way up the Creag. Stopping at the top of the hill to catch her breath, she looked out across the moor toward Auld Mary's cottage. But it was a gray, misty day and she could not see it. Martha hoped she would not lose her way. She had never gone so far by herself. Mum would not mind, as long as she did not go near the peat bog beyond Auld Mary's hut.

The grass beneath her feet was wet, though it had not rained today. Cook always said a Scots mist would wet an Englishman to the skin. It was that kind of day, when the air itself seemed damp. The purple bells of the heather glistened with dew, and the long grass clung wetly to Martha's legs. A corncrake called out in its raspy voice, *crek crek*, and took to the sky in flight. The chestnut patches on its wings stood out brightly against the gray sky.

Halfway to Auld Mary's hut was a lonely pine tree. Martha could see it, its blue-green needles rattling in the wind. Once she reached it, she had but to follow the curve of a hill to get to Auld Mary's door.

Suddenly there it was, a tiny mud-and-turf cottage with smoke drifting out of a hole in the roof. The cottage had a friendly sort of look about it. Tangled vines framed the open doorway, with a few late roses showing off their silken petals. An orange cat with very white paws sat in the doorway, staring at Martha and twitching its tail.

Now that she was here Martha felt a little shy. She had known Auld Mary all her life, but it was different, somehow, coming here to ask for magic. She wondered if Auld Mary was really a witch. Cook had all kinds of stories about witches who did fearful things like make crops fail and animals fall sick. They flew about at night on broomsticks and sent their cats around to spy on people. Suppose . . .

But no. Auld Mary had been there when Martha was born. Father would never let anyone wicked come near one of his bairns. Martha's chin went up and she said in a firm voice, "Hullo, cat."

The cat opened its mouth and yawned a very wide yawn. Then it turned and went into the hut.

Martha followed it slowly. In the doorway she called out, "Good day!" but there was no answer.

She took another step forward.

"Auld Mary?" she asked.

Auld Mary was not there. Martha and the cat were alone in the hut. It was a tiny house with just one dark room. For a moment Martha could not see anything but the peat fire smoldering inside a ring of hearthstones in the middle of the dirt floor.

Then her eyes got used to the dim light. She could see a spinning wheel, a water pail, and an earthen bench built against one wall. On top of the bench was a thick woven blanket spread out over a pile of straw. That was Auld Mary's bed.

Against another wall was a second bench. It held an empty dye pot, some dishes and bottles, and a small bag of meal. Slumped against the meal was a little muslin doll with no face. Martha remembered that Auld Mary sometimes made dolls to trade for meat. They were only rag dolls, not painted wooden dolls with real glass eyes like Lady Flora.

Bunches of dried plants and herbs hung upside-down all along the rafters, as well as a braid of onions and some rush baskets. A small iron pot hung from a hook over the fire. Something inside it bubbled gently. It smelled like potatoes. Beside the fire were two short-legged stools and one long bench, which had upon it two rough wooden plates and two cups and a dish of oatcakes. The cakes looked just baked. Martha suddenly realized she was very hungry, even though she had eaten dinner not long ago. It had been a long walk.

"Ah, I see ye've caught yerself a mouse, Kitty!"

Martha turned at the sound of the voice. There was Auld Mary, wrinkled and bent and dressed in an ancient shirtwaist and a coarse gray skirt. A yellowing linen cap covered her head, and her plaid apron was faded and dull from many washings. But the light wool shawl around her shoulders was fluffy and creamy-white, knitted in the most delicate, lacy stitches. Mum said no one in Glencaraid could knit so well as Auld Mary.

The cat ran over and rubbed against Auld Mary's legs, mewing loudly.

"Aye, not bein' blind, I can see for meself 'tis a fine big mouse," Auld Mary told it reproachfully.

Martha looked around but she did not see any mouse. She wondered if perhaps Auld Mary had not seen her yet. But the old woman turned a beaming eye upon her and said, "A red-headed mouse, me favorite kind!" So Martha knew she was the mouse.

She swallowed and said in a small voice,

"Good day to you, ma'am."

"Put this on the bench, there's a lass," Auld Mary said, handing Martha a basket that was covered with a handkerchief. "I'll just see to oor liddle bit o' dinner."

Martha could not speak. She set the basket beside the oatcakes, wondering what was inside it. She stood still and watched as Auld Mary took the pot off the fire and poured its contents onto a pile of heather on the dirt floor. The water drained through and soaked into the dirt, leaving four small potatoes steaming on top of the heather.

Auld Mary picked up two knitting needles and used them to lift a potato onto each plate. It seemed to Martha a very odd thing to do. Then she saw that there were no knives or forks on the table.

"Well, be you hungry or be you not?" Auld Mary asked, setting a little pot of honey next to the oatcakes. She motioned for Martha to take a seat on one of the stools. Martha stared. It was almost as if Auld Mary had known she was coming.

People did say Auld Mary had the second sight. Perhaps she really could see into the future, and knew what was going to happen before it actually happened. Then she would already know why Martha was here. Suddenly Martha felt a great leap of excitement. Maybe that was what was in the covered basket! Perhaps Auld Mary had already gone out to pick the magic plant that would make Martha grow faster!

Martha felt her shyness melt away. She sat on the stool and hungrily ate the steaming boiled potatoes and the crisp oatcakes spread with clover honey. There was no butter but the bread didn't need it.

"Tell me ye've ivver tasted better honey in yer life, and I'll tell ye ye're a liar," Auld Mary said cheerfully.

Martha did not need to worry about being called a liar. It was the most delicious honey she had ever tasted. Auld Mary said she had collected it herself from the best hive in the glen.

It was fun to eat the potatoes the way Auld

Mary did, picking them up whole with her fingers and biting off a chunk the way she might take bites from an apple. Cook's potatoes were much tastier, for she salted them, but luckily Auld Mary did not ask if Martha had tasted better potatoes.

Talking to Auld Mary was not like talking to anyone else Martha knew. The old woman spoke to the cat as much as to Martha, and she paused and nodded as if he were answering her back. When she did speak to Martha, it was as though Martha dropped by for dinner every day. Auld Mary did not seem to think it a bit unusual that Martha had walked all the way out here by herself. She did not ask why Martha had come. She only asked questions about how things were in the Stone House, and Martha found herself chattering away in reply.

She told Auld Mary about how the new bairn was getting on, and the christening procession, and the letter Mum had gotten from Uncle Harry, saying that he was bringing Aunt Grisell and all the cousins to visit for a whole month in the winter. She told her about Duncan's Latin lessons and the boil on Sandy's neck. But all the time she was bursting to ask what was in the basket, and how fast it would make her grow big.

"Tell that Sandy to send one o' his bairns to me an' I'll gie him an ointment to take awa that boil," Auld Mary said. "Send it hame wi' ye today, I would, only it's got to be mixed in the full o' the moon and that's no till the morrow's night."

Still Auld Mary had not said anything about what was inside the basket. The potatoes were finished and the oatcakes were gone. Auld Mary put the oatcake crumbs on the floor for the orange cat. It leaned against Martha's leg in a nice purry sort of way as it licked up the last tiny bits of bread.

"It's wonderin' I am if ye've room in that wee belly for a liddle treat," said Auld Mary.

"A treat!" Martha said, surprised. The clover honey had been treat enough.

"Aye," said Auld Mary. "I up an' picked these as soon as ever I knew ye was comin'."

She took the handkerchief off the basket. Martha's heart thumped. Then Auld Mary tipped the basket to show Martha the plump purple berries inside.

"Bilberries?" Martha's voice was very small.

"Sure as day." The wrinkled face beamed at Martha. "Th' season's gettin' a mite long in th' tooth for berries, but I kenned there'd be some late hangers-on in that liddle sheltered holler around back o' th' hill. Hied me there the second I saw yer bonny self trippin' cross th' moor, I did."

"Oh," Martha said. She could not think of anything else to say. She knew she ought to be grateful about the bilberries—a whole big basket, and only one person to share them with. But they were just plain ordinary bilberries. They would not make her grow big enough to use the spinning wheel. She would have to wait until she was older, just as Grisie had done.

And if Auld Mary had the second sight, she had not used it to know Martha was coming. She had only seen her walking toward the cottage.

"Now ye'll no be tryin' to tell me ye've nae taste for bilberries, Mouse," said Auld Mary suddenly. "All mice likes berries. It must be somethin' else troublin' ye. I wish ye'd tell me and Kitty here what it is. I'm nae great shakes at dishin' oot advice, meself, but Kitty's been around a long time and he kens a thing or two."

The orange cat meowed and jumped into Auld Mary's lap. Martha looked into the cat's golden eyes and then into the sharp, bright eyes of Auld Mary. Suddenly she found herself telling the whole story. Auld Mary listened and the cat listened. When Martha was done the cat licked its paw and nuzzled Auld Mary's chin and leaped down to the floor. It ran out of the house, its long tail waving straight up in the air.

Auld Mary laughed. "The cowardly beast. Canna face tellin' ye the ill news."

Martha swallowed. "Ill news?" The hope that had begun to flicker inside her sighed and went out.

"Aye," Auld Mary said, but her eyes were

twinkling. "He kens there's no a plant nor beast on earth can make a wee lass grow before her time. But—" The uncanny green eyes smiled at Martha. "There's mair than one way to shear a sheep. I'll teach ye to spin as I learned when I was no mair than yer size."

"Truly?" Martha cried. "But how did you reach the treadle?"

"Leave ye the treadle-wheel for them as likes to sit by the fire," said Auld Mary. "Ye've not muckle taste for stayin' put, anyhow, have ye, Mouse? I've seen ye flittin' aboot the hills. Like the wind ye are, nivver at rest if ye can help it."

Martha nodded slowly, thinking. It was true that what she hated most about sewing was the sitting still. Spinning meant long spells in one chair, too. She had not thought about it before. But then how was Auld Mary going to teach her?

Before she could ask, Auld Mary went to a basket in the corner and rummaged around. She came back with a funny-looking wooden stick that had a round wooden disk at one end.

Auld Mary read the question in Martha's eyes. "'Tis a spindle. When I was a bairn nivver would ye see a lass oot walkin' wi'oot one. Spun all the time, we did, while we were aye mindin' the cows or takin' the air."

She ran a finger along the spindle's length and smiled fondly at it. "Noo all the world has turned to spinnin' wheels, and sure it's no I who'd wish them away. A good wheel spins a heap mair thread in th' same spot o' time. Nivver spin enough to earn me bread, I would, if I had to do it all wi' a spindle. But—"

She held the spindle out to Martha, who took it gingerly. It did not look like much, just an old smooth stick stuck through a wooden circle.

Auld Mary went on. "A month's practice wi' this, Mouse, and ye'll be spinnin' yarn jist as fine as anything yer sister Grisie can make on her wheel. And by the time ye've grown big enough to take up the wheel yerself, yer fingers'll ken exactly what to do already an' ye'll have the wheel doon pat in the shake of a lamb's tail."

Martha gave a sudden grin. "That'd be grand," she said.

"Ye'll no want to start wi' flax, though," Auld Mary said. "Wool's a sight easier for wee fingers."

Auld Mary took a bit of brushed, combed wool from the bench near her spinning wheel. She showed Martha how to draw out a few woolly hairs and loop them around a piece of string she had tied onto the spindle, just below the round wooden disk. Auld Mary said the disk was called a whorl.

"The string is just to get ye started," she explained. "Noo watch this."

Holding on to the wool she had looped through the string, Auld Mary let the spindle dangle in the air. With her free hand, she set the spindle spinning. The weight of the whorl kept the spindle twirling like a top. As it turned, it twisted the woolly hairs into one tight piece of thread. Auld Mary gently pulled more hairs out from the bit of wool in her hand—it was just like drawing out the strands of flax from Mum's distaff, Martha

realized—and allowed the whirling spindle to continue twisting the strands into thread.

That was all there was to it, Auld Mary said. When she had spun an arm's length of thread, Auld Mary wrapped it around the base of the spindle just above the whorl. Then she held Martha's hands to show her how to draw out new strands of wool as she set the spindle spinning again.

The wool was softer than the flax had been, and rather greasy. It took a lot of practice before Martha could do it by herself. Sometimes the thread broke and the spindle fell to the ground. Then Auld Mary had to help Martha loop the thread onto the spindle again.

But before she left Auld Mary's house Martha had spun enough thread to wind into a small ball. It was very thick thread and had almost as many slubs and wide fuzzy patches as the thread she had spun on Mum's wheel. Auld Mary said not to worry; she would soon learn the trick of keeping it smooth and even. It was fun to watch the spindle whirling around in the air, and Martha felt very proud to see the ball of thread she had made. Auld Mary said she must keep it, and the spindle as well.

"'Twas only yesterday it was tellin' me it had a hankering to travel," she said.

"I don't think spindles can talk," Martha said.

For some reason this made Auld Mary laugh and laugh. "Ye dinna, do ye? And hoo does a mouse come to ken so much about spindles, when she nivver laid eyes on one before today?"

Martha could not think of an answer. Auld Mary laughed again and reached for the basket of bilberries.

"Ye'd best stick to what ye ken, Mouse— like berries! Come noo, ye must eat these up afore ye scoot on home. Gettin' on toward suppertime, it is, and yer mither will wonder where ye've got to!"

Martha was astonished. The afternoon had gone so quickly. When the berries were gone, she thanked Auld Mary and promised to come visit her again. The orange cat appeared in the doorway just as she was leaving, and rubbed against her leg as if to say it hoped everything had turned out all right.

All the long way home Martha tried to practice with the spindle. It was harder to do while she was walking. Auld Mary had said she must learn to spin standing still first. She would practice and practice, Martha told herself, until she could do it perfectly, even while she was moving about. She would take the spindle with her everywhere, and soon her thread would come out fine and even. None of her family could spin thread while walking. Not even Grisie.

The Fairy Spindle

Mum said Martha was a lucky girl to be given the use of such a fine old spindle.

"It must mean a great deal to Auld Mary, if she kept it all these years," Mum said, turning the shiny wood over in her hands. "You must take great care with it, Martha."

Martha nodded solemnly. It was strange to think that Auld Mary had used this very same spindle when she was a little girl. Auld Mary was so old that it did not seem like she could ever have been young. She would not have been called Auld Mary then, just Mary. Martha wondered when people had starting putting the "Auld" in front of her name.

Mum gave Martha a bundle of combed wool for her very own. "I think it's a fine idea for you to gain skill on the spindle. I played with one meself, from time to time, when I was a lass. But I never learned the trick of spinning while I was walking about. All our maids could do it, and the old women on the land, but hand spindles were thought too common for young ladies to use."

Every day after that Martha took her wool to the garden and practiced and practiced. She liked the way the spindle whirled in the air like a fairy top. She liked the crinkly feel of the wool. She pretended that Lady Flora was a great lady in a grand old castle with fifteen bedrooms, and Martha was her maidservant spinning fine woolen yarn for the household stores. When the spindle became too heavy with yarn to use, she took the yarn off and rolled it into a ball.

The yarn she rolled into a second ball was

beginning to look like proper thread. There were not as many slubs. Martha could not yet keep the spindle from wobbling out of control while she was walking about, but when she sat still she could spin yarn that was smooth and straight, nothing like the lumpy strand she had spun on Mum's wheel. Mum said that this was yarn she would be proud to use.

And Grisie said, "Why, 'tis grand fine yarn you've made, Martha!" She did not say "for a wee thing."

At the end of a month, when Martha had spun enough to wind a third ball, Grisie said, "You've enough there to knit up a doll blanket. I'll help you, if you like."

An idea flashed into Martha's head. "I want to make mittens," she said. "For Laird Alroch."

"Truly?" Grisie seemed surprised. Martha nodded her head firmly, and Grisie shrugged. "I suppose you could. You've certainly got enough yarn for it, and a good thick yarn it is. It would make fine warm mittens. But whatever made you think of giving mittens to Laird Alroch? It's been aye two months since he was here."

Martha shrugged. She did not want to tell Grisie about the dust-gown, or why she wanted to do something nice for the old laird. "He is coming for Hogmanay, isna he?"

Hogmanay was the biggest celebration of the year. It came on the last day of the year, and there would be singing and feasting until midnight and beyond. Uncle Harry and his family would be visiting then, and Martha had heard Mum say they must find another bed for Laird Alroch.

"Aye, he'll be with us. Still, it's a funny notion. I dinna ken where you get your ideas, Martha."

"From me head," Martha answered. "Same as most people."

Mum said Martha might work on the mittens in the mornings instead of her sewing sampler. But she must practice her sewing twice a week, so that her fingers would not lose the skill they had gained. Martha liked knitting much better. She could not prick herself on a knitting needle. Grisie sat beside her and helped her to make the thumbs. They worked in Mum and Father's cozy bedroom, where the peats were always blazing warm now. It was autumn, and the weather was growing cold.

The Stone House was ready for the coming winter. Outside the peats were stacked high against the stone walls. All the oats had been harvested from Father's fields, and the barley and peas and beans. The grain had been taken down to Clachan to be ground into meal. Now the big barrels of oatmeal stood in a row along the kitchen wall, like stout wooden soldiers. Potatoes had been sewn into sacks for storage, and there were baskets and baskets of turnips and cabbages to eat during the long winter.

Many more turnips had been saved for the cows to eat, for the shaggy long-haired cattle had been brought down from the shieling, fat from their summer's grazing. Drovers had come to drive some of Father's cattle to the faraway town of Falkirk, where the big cattle fair was held. The money from the cattle would buy sugar and wine and spices, and even some wheat flour that could be baked into real wheaten bread for special occasions. It would also pay for Alisdair and Robbie and Duncan's books and schooling fees.

After the cattle sale, Father and Sandy rode to Perth, the biggest town in the county, to buy supplies. Martha wished she could go too. She wanted to see the great ships coming into the port at the Firth of Tay, loaded with cotton from America. She wanted to see the shops and the fishing boats and the crowds of people. But Father said it was no kind of trip for a small lass to make. She had to stay home with Mum and the rest, watching the lake road, until one afternoon Father's horse came into sight, with Sandy behind him on a horse loaded down with supplies. That evening Cook made a special supper of the salmon Father had brought home, and a wheaten loaf, and a cup of tea for everyone, even Martha.

Dark came earlier now. Each evening at suppertime Mum lit the oil lamps in the bedroom. The peats glowed orange and the lamps glowed yellow, and shadows danced and flickered about the room. After supper came the time when Mum told stories. The boys roasted nuts on the fire-grate, and Father sat in his big chair beside the fire to listen.

Sometimes Mum told about when she was a little girl living with her auntie on the Isle of Skye, far away off the western coast of Scotland. Other times she told stories about Bonnie Prince Charlie, who had fought for the crown of Scotland many years ago, before Father and Mum were born. Martha liked to hear about the dashing prince who had rallied an army of Highlanders and gone bravely to battle against the British king. The prince's army believed that Prince Charlie, and not the British King George II, should sit on the throne of Scotland. Mum's own father had fought in that war. Although Prince Charlie had lost, Martha thought he was brave to try.

But Martha's favorite stories of all were fairy tales. One night, as Mum wound a skein of newly spun linen thread off the bobbin, she said it put her in mind of a story her auntie used to tell.

"It was called 'The Crofter's Daughter and the Wedding Dress,'" Mum said, "and it went like this."

There once was a poor crofter who farmed a small bit of land in a bare stony glen. He made but a meager living, and some years he stored away scarcely enough meal to keep his family from starving in the winter. But he had a light heart and a merry way about him, for he was the sort o' man who merely tightened his belt and whistled all the louder when hunger knocked at his door.

As men will do, he had married a wife who was as like to him as wet is to dry. Never was there a moment when she was not all a-flutter with worry over this and over that. In the winter she worried that the peats wouldna burn, and in summer she worried that the thatch in the roof would catch fire from a spark and burn up over their heads. She worried about the crops and the hens and the weather, and most of all she worried that her daughter would never find a husband.

Now, this daughter was as bonny a lass as the hills have ever seen. She had her father's way of looking for the good in a thing, and over and over she did tell her mother not to worry about a silly thing like a husband.

"If I'm to marry, a husband will find me," she would say to her mother, "as sure as rain finds its way to the soil."

"Husbands dinna fall from the sky like rain!" her mother would cry.

"Aye, and 'tis a good thing," laughed the lass, "for whatever we'd do with them all after a storm, I canna say!"

Sure and the girl was right not to worry, for it was just that laughter rippling down the hillside that caught the ear of a young man on his way across the valley. He was a fine, smart lad who was headed over the mountain to run the farm his uncle had left him. When he heard the laugh of the crofter's daughter, as sweet and light as silver bells chiming on the wind, he said to himself: That's a voice a man could be happy to listen to for the rest of his life. And when he caught sight of the lass, with her merry eyes and her shining red hair, he said to himself: There's the very girl for me. He introduced himself to the mother, and pointed out that they were to be neighbors of a sort. Then he asked if he might have a drink of water before he headed up the mountain to the farm waiting for him on the other side.

The mother gave him a long look. She took in his kind, honest face, and his callused hands that showed he was not afraid of work, and finally she said, "Aye, ye'll get that," and went into the cottage to fill a cup for the lad. For once in her life she felt almost like laughing aloud herself, for she could see that the lad was that taken with her daughter, and the daughter was chattering away with the lad as if they were born friends. The mother thought to herself that here was as fine a husband as she could wish for her daughter, and him with a farm just across the mountain, too!

So she brought out the water, and she brought out bannocks and the bit of butter she'd been saving for the Sunday meal. Then, being wise about some things for all she was such a foolish worrier about most, she stayed back near the cottage and let the young people talk and eat and laugh together on the sunny hillside. And sure as day, before the afternoon was gone the two young people were fast in love with each other.

At last the young man stirred himself to get on with his journey, and he made his good-byes. But a week later he was back again, and every week after that, and so it was no surprise to the mother that a day came when the lad asked the crofter for the daughter's hand in marriage. The crofter knew the lad well by this time and was aye glad to see his daughter make such a fine match. So the lad and lass were happy, and the crofter was happy, and the mother ought to have been the happiest of all.

But as soon as the wedding plans were made, the mother's worries began again. Now she fretted from sunup to sundown about how she should ever find the means to make her daughter's wedding dress. There was hardly enough flax that year to spin linen for sheets, and as the girl pointed out to her mother, a bride must have at least one set of sheets to carry to her husband's house. And a dress could not be bought, either, for coins were scarce as hen's teeth in the crofter's house.

"Me Sunday frock will serve me fine for a wedding dress, Mother," said the girl, but it only made her mother fret the more. Day after day the mother sighed and moaned and wrung her hands. Her worries took such a hold on her that her health began to fail.

Then the lass felt a spark of worry herself. She mightn't agree with her mother, but she loved her all the same. She vowed to herself that she would find a way to make a wedding dress that would cheer her mother's heart.

She went out alone on the hillside to think about it. The warm sun shone down upon her and the wind teased at her hair and her skirts. A little stream ran down the hill and it bubbled and laughed beside her, as glad a sound as any the lass had ever heard. But for the first time in her life, the girl did not laugh along. Instead she bit her lip and wrinkled her brow and set herself to think.

At last she said to herself: If we haven't the flax, I must find something else to spin. She took her spindle out of her pocket and tried to twist a few blades of grass into yarn, but that didna work. She tried with some heather, but that didna work. She tried with some broom, but neither did that work.

In the end she threw herself down in the grass and might even have cried from the hopelessness of it, if a wee strange noise had not come to her ear. It was a sound a bit like a cricket chirping and a bit like a bird peeping, and most of all like someone crying. The lass looked all around, but she saw nothing. Then she decided the noise was coming from inside a gorse-bush—happen it was a rabbit or a bird that had hurt itself. Having a heart as kind as it was merry, she looked inside the bush to see if she could help the poor creature.

To her great surprise, there in the gorse was a tiny, tiny lass, weeping her poor heart out. The crofter's daughter saw at a glance that here was one of the Wee Folk, and she stared a moment in wonder at the beautiful fairy lass. She wore a bodice of golden silk, bright as the sun, and a blue skirt of a cloth that rippled to the ground like water flowing over stones. Her shawl was of lacy white gauze, so light and airy that it danced around the fairy in a cloud as she sobbed.

The crofter's daughter gasped to see such a lovely and pitiful sight.

Then the fairy looked up with a start. Caution filled her strange golden eyes, but the sorrow she bore was too great to be surprised out of her. She gave a deep shuddering sob and buried her head in her hands again.

"But whatever is the matter?" asked the crofter's lass.

"Och, what matters it to you?" sobbed the fairy.

"Happen I can help," said the lass, and at that the fairy looked up again and gave a bitter laugh through her tears.

"Very well, I'll tell ye," the fairy said. 'Twas clear she did not put much stock in the advice a simple crofter's daughter could give her, but the Wee Folk, same as mortals, do ever have a liking for talking about their own selves. "'Tis my wedding day a month from now, and I've nothing to wear but this old sorry frock I've worn for more seasons than a mortal could count!"

"But it's lovely!" gasped the crofter's daughter. "Nivver in me life have I seen a gown so fine!"

The fairy's eyes filled with scorn, and a scornful hand plucked at her bodice. "This? Why, 'tis nothing the poorest among us would look twice at! Anyone can snatch a few sunbeams and spin them into yarn. A fairy's wedding dress must be something rare and beautiful, not anything so common as this!"

The crofter's daughter gasped again. "The thread in your bodice is spun of sunlight? It canna be possible! But there, that *would* explain why it has such a lovely glow to it. And your skirt?"

"Water, of course," said the fairy impatiently. "And my shawl is spun from a bit of wind, as any fool can see. Now you understand why I canna be married in such a common frock!"

"Nay," said the lass. "I dinna understand at all. A queen would give all her riches for that gown you've got on!"

The fairy rolled her eyes. "A mortal queen, you mean. Any fairy worth her mettle must think of something that's never been turned into cloth before. I was going to spin the thread out of fire—there's no color I would look so well in as flame— but I've just found out my groom can't abide the smell of smoke! Am I to have him sneezing all over me at the wedding feast, then?" She burst into a fresh round of sobs.

The crofter's daughter bit her lip again, thinking. The fairy went on sobbing and the sun went on shining and the water in the stream kept up its bubbling laugh. The wind tickled a lock of hair into the eyes of the farmer's daughter, and as she brushed it back into place, an idea came to her.

"I hope I'm no makin' too bold," said the lass, "but happen ye could have your flame-colored gown after all. By chance would a lock of my hair serve as thread for your cloth?"

Now it was the fairy's turn to gasp, and

she stared at the lass in wonder. The lass's red hair with the sun glinting upon it did indeed glow like fire.

" 'Twould be the very thing," murmured the fairy, and a smile lit up her face.

So the lass cut off a lock of her hair and tied it fast with a bit of thread. She gave it to the fairy, saying, "Take it, and I wish you as much joy in your marriage as I hope to find in mine."

"Are you to be married also?" cried the fairy. "Then you must let me help with your wedding dress! 'Tis only fair! What sort of a frock are you to be married in?"

Then the lass told her all about the shortage of flax, and the shortage of money, and how she had come out to the hill to try to spin herself some thread out of grass or heather or broom.

"I wish I had your skill with spinning!" said the lass. "To think you can capture a sunbeam upon your spindle, and weave brook water into cloth!"

The fairy laughed. "You mortals are a

curious lot. If you truly want a dress like mine, I can spin you the thread in the blink of an eye!"

And sure enough, the fairy reached up and caught hold of a sunray. She took out a little spindle, and quicker than quick, she turned that sunbeam into a shimmering golden thread. Then she dipped her hand into the stream and brought some of the clean, cool water to her spindle. The spindle whirled round and soon the fairy had spun a skein of thread as blue as a summer lake. And at the last, she simply held the spindle in the air and let it spin around in the breeze. So quickly that the crofter's daughter could scarce believe it, the fairy had spun a skein of airy white thread that was finer than anything the lass had ever seen before.

"For your veil," said the fairy, and she gave all the thread to the lass. Then, taking up the flame-red lock of hair, the fairy said good-bye to the girl and *pop!* she disappeared.

The girl took her thread home to her mother and told her all about the wee fairy. The mother was amazed, and when she had woven the thread into cloth she shook her head in wonder, for never was there a mortal bride more lovely than the crofter's daughter. After that the crofter's wife made up her mind not to fret and worry anymore. Who could be fretful with a daughter so sweet and merry that she charmed even the fairy folk? When the wedding day came around, the crofter's cottage was so filled with laughter that it echoed down the glen, and the wedding supper was the merriest the valley had ever known.

"Tell it again!" Martha cried when Mum had finished. Mum laughed and said once was enough for now. The fire danced and crackled. A fire was a kind of magic, just like Auld Mary's spindle was a kind of magic. The fairy's spindle in the story was yet another kind. Martha looked at the fire, and she looked at Mum, busy at the spinning wheel. She looked at Father, holding a book open upon his knee, with his hair all spiky where he had run his hands through it after taking off his wig.

Mothers and fathers, Martha thought, had their own kind of magic.

The Riddle

Harvest was over. The boys were back in school. Grisie had her fifteenth birthday, and she began to put up her hair. She looked so grown-up that for a few days Martha almost felt shy around her, as if Grisie were a visiting lady instead of the big sister she had known all her life. But when Alisdair and Robbie teased Grisie about how she would soon have to start looking for a husband, Grisie blushed and snapped at them to go dunk their heads in the loch. Then Martha knew it was just Grisie after all.

"Will Grisie really find a husband soon?" Martha asked Mum.

"Whisht!" Mum said. "I should think not. She's but a lass yet. Dinna you hearken to your brothers. Lads will tease, and sheep will baa, and a wise man sets his clock by neither one."

A few days after Grisie's birthday, just as dinner was ending, Father looked out the window and smiled. He said he had a surprise, and it was coming up the hill.

"Someone's coming to visit?" asked Duncan.

"Uncle Harry!" Robbie crowed.

Father laughed and shook his head. "It's but October, Robert. You ken as well as I that Harry and his lot aren't expected until December."

"Och, I mind it now," Robbie said ruefully. "Then who is it?"

"I'll give you a hint," said Father. "'Tis no a 'who,' but aye a 'what.' And here's another clue:

*"A mouth full o' teeth that sings with no
   tongue.
A shelf full o' keys that open no locks.
As old as a wood, as young as a bairn,
All the air in the world caught fast in a
   box."*

Martha clapped her hands. She loved it when Father told riddles. It was a game he played when he was especially pleased about something. She did not know what the surprise was, but it must be something very nice.

Everyone was quiet, searching for the answer to the riddle. The sound of wheels rumbling came through the window. Was it a carriage or a wagon? Martha wanted to run and look, but she knew that would spoil the game. Father smiled at Mum across the table. Mum's eyes snapped with merriment. She knew the answer already.

"What is it, Mum?" Martha whispered.

"I'll not tell! Come, let's have some guesses."

"A cage of monkeys, like in our picture book," Robbie said.

Father's big laugh rang out. "That *would* be a surprise! How did you come to that, lad?"

"Mon*keys* could be keys that open no locks," Robbie said. "Donkeys, too, I suppose. Some of them could be very old and some very young."

"A good try. But what of the other two lines in the riddle?"

Robbie gave up and laughed along with everyone else. "I dinna ken," he said. "But I'd like to have a monkey."

"We've enough monkeys in this house, I think," Mum teased.

"Alisdair?" Father asked. "Have you a guess?"

Alisdair bit his lip thoughtfully. "A river with a lot of rocks in it could be the mouth full of teeth that sings with no tongue. And a river could be as old as a wood but have raindrops in it that would be as young as a bairn. But I don't see where the keys would come in, nor the air in the box."

"Anyway, how could a river be coming up

the hill right now?" Grisie asked.

"Aye," Alisdair said. "That troubled me too."

"What say you, Grisie?" Father asked.

Grisie shook her head. "All I could think of was a cage of birds, but they have tongues with no teeth, not the other way around. And they dinna make sense with the rest o' it, anyhow."

The rumbling sound was louder and then suddenly it stopped. The wheels had rolled into the yard.

"Hullo, the house!" cried a voice from outside.

"Good guesses, all, though none of them were right," said Father, rising to his feet. "Happen we should gang outside to see the answer. 'Tis glad I am we've a dry afternoon for once."

He led the way downstairs, with Mum on his arm. Everyone crowded into the doorway. Martha could see nothing but the backs of her brothers and sister.

Duncan said, "Let Martha in front. She's

the littlest." Martha smiled at him gratefully and wriggled to the front. A wagon was in the yard, with a very large something in the back, wrapped in canvas and tied all over with rope. She still did not know what it could be.

Father went to talk to the wagon driver. Then he sent Robbie to get Sandy and some other men to help unload whatever was in the wagon box. It took a long time for the men to cut the ropes and lift the huge wrapped bundle to the ground. It made a strange chiming noise when they set it down.

"Look sharp, there!" Father called. "It's delicate."

Martha felt nearly wild with impatience to know what it was. At last the men began to lift off the canvas. Grisie sucked in her breath, and everyone stood silent for a moment.

It was a pianoforte, and you could play music on it. It was made of gleaming red-brown wood and stood on four beautifully carved legs. Grisie began to cry.

"Och, Father!" she said wonderingly. "I canna believe it's real. Are we truly to keep it?"

"Aye." Father beamed with satisfaction. "I've had it shipped all the way from Perth. You shall learn to play, and so shall Martha."

Martha clapped her hands.

"But who will teach us?" asked Grisie.

Mum lifted up the wooden case that covered the keys. Everyone crowded close to try pressing them down.

"'Tis no so different from the spinet I played when I was a lass," Mum said. "I can teach you a little. And later we'll get someone in to give you proper lessons. It's getting on to the time for us to find a governess for Martha, anyway, in another year or so."

Martha was surprised. She had forgotten that she would have a governess someday. Her cousins had a young lady living with them to teach them arithmetic and lace making and drawing. It would be strange to have another person living in the Stone House, teaching her those things.

But she did not have time to think about it, for Alisdair cried out, "I see it now! The pianoforte keys are the keys that dinna open locks! And they're the teeth, too, that sing without a tongue when you play music on them."

"Good lad," said Father. "What for the rest of it?"

Alisdair was thoughtful. "Well, a pianoforte is made of wood, so it's old as a wood. But it's young, too, for it was just built. Right?"

"Aye," Father said.

"But I don't understand the last part. It's aye a box, I see that, but how does it hold all the air in the world?"

Duncan pressed some of the keys, one at a time, and it made a funny little tune. Suddenly Martha knew what the last line of the riddle meant.

"It's air like a song!" she cried out. "A song is called an air."

Alisdair's eyes lit up. "Aye, and you can play all the songs in the world on a pianoforte!"

Father lifted Martha off the ground and hugged her. "That's my smart lass! You shall choose the first air your mother is to play, when once we get it inside."

The pianoforte was moved into the parlor near the front window. It had a little stool with a round seat and carved legs. Mum sat down upon it and put her fingers on the keys.

All that afternoon the family clustered around the pianoforte and listened to Mum play. She played slowly at first, stumbling over the notes, and then more and more smoothly. The pianoforte had a very different feel than the spinet, she said. She could not thump the keys so hard as she had when she was a girl playing the spinet, lest she break the pianoforte's more delicate strings.

Now the days when Duncan was in school did not seem so long to Martha. She had the pianoforte to play on, and Auld Mary's spindle to spin with. When it was Grisie's turn at the pianoforte, Martha tucked her wool under her arm and marched around the parlor in time to the music. Little by little, she began to be able to spin while she was moving. Sometimes Grisie hit a wrong note and then Martha would jump and a slub would slip into the yarn. Grisie laughed and said that she had put more mistakes into Martha's spinning than Martha had herself.

Now, sometimes after supper the family sat in the parlor, singing and listening to the pianoforte. Mum taught Martha to play "Wee Willie Gray" and "The Old Man in the Wood." Grisie knew six tunes already; Father said she was a born musician. He said he was proud of all his songbirds, who kept the house brimming with music.

The Boat

At last Laird Alroch's mittens were finished. They were warm and sturdy with only a few missed stitches, and the right hand was very nearly the same size as the left. Father tried them on and said he had no doubt Laird Alroch would be proud to wear them.

"Happen one of these days you'll knit me a pair, lass," he said to Martha. Martha felt very proud, and she wished she could begin work on Father's mittens right away. But first, she had decided to make some for Auld Mary, to thank her for the use of the spindle. And after that she wanted to make a shawl for Lady Flora to wear for the holidays. Mum had a whole fleece saved in the attic that had been bleached snowy white last summer, and she said Martha might have a bit to do with as she liked. It would have to be a very little piece of the fleece, but when spun into thread there would be just enough for Martha to make an elegant little wrap for Lady Flora's shoulders. Lady Flora must have new clothes for Hogmanay.

Everyone was to have a new suit of clothes for the holidays. Mum sent a load of linen and wool yarns to the weaver in Clachan to be made into different kinds of cloth. There was a lot of dyed green linen that Mum said would be just the thing for Martha's new dress. She said there ought to be enough left over to make a little matching gown for Lady Flora.

"Truly?" Martha squealed.

"Aye, but you'll have the hemming of the skirt yourself."

When the finished cloth came back from

the weaver, Mum spread it out and looked it over carefully. After a long time she nodded in satisfaction.

"There's naught better than Angus Cameron for turning out a good sturdy cloth," she said. "That damask Father brought back from Perth was not so well made as this, for all it was so fancy."

After that Mum and Grisie were busy sewing every day nearly from sunup to sundown. Martha worked beside them, knitting Auld Mary's mittens and then Lady Flora's shawl. Martha's new green dress was soon ready. The high waist was belted with a sash of tartan plaid, with stripes of red and green and gold crisscrossing each other. The sleeves and hem were trimmed with golden ribbons Mum had cut from one of her old silk dresses. The little matching gown for Lady Flora had its own wee ribbons around the sleeves and bodice, and there were tiny rosettes above each flounce of the skirt.

Martha liked to look at that skirt. The hem had not taken so long to sew as she had feared, and the stitches came very near to marching in a straight line. She could not wait to dress Lady Flora in the lovely gown on Hogmanay morning. The golden ribbons were just the color of Flora's shining hair, and the little pink rosettes matched her cheeks. The gown was so pretty that it was almost a shame to cover it with the woolly shawl Martha had knit, and she decided to put that on the doll only when she took her outside.

It was too cold to spend much time outdoors, though. Snow had made its own white shawl for the fields and the garden and the hillsides. Everyone stayed close to the fire, telling stories and playing winter games.

Mollie and Nannie were as busy with cleaning as Mum was with sewing. All the floors must be scoured with sand, and all the furniture rubbed with a cloth to make the wood gleam. The beds must be aired and pillows made for all the guests who were soon to arrive.

Whenever Grisie had a bit of spare time, she sat at the pianoforte, practicing and practicing. She wanted to play for Aunt Grisell and

Uncle Harry when they arrived on Hogmanay. Everyone was looking forward to the New Year's Eve celebration. Martha found it hard to think of anything else. There would be singing and dancing and presents and everyone's favorite foods. And the day after, New Year's Day, was Martha's birthday. She would be seven years old. That was one year closer to being old enough to search for the water fairy in Robbie's boat.

One night when Martha went to bed, she got Grisie to help her count the days till Hogmanay. Six more days.

Then it was five days, and four, and then three. The day before Hogmanay, Cook said it was time to make the haggis. That was Martha's favorite food of all, and Cook had said Martha might help her prepare it. Martha went straight to the kitchen after breakfast, but Cook shooed her out.

"I'll not be ready for hours yet! Go on wi' ye and play until I call ye."

Martha went back upstairs. She could not think of anything to do. She thought she would try Flora's new dress on her one more time. Just yesterday Grisie had surprised her with a little ruffled petticoat for Lady Flora that matched Martha's new one.

Duncan came in, his cheeks red with cold.

"Martha! There you are. You must come and see what I've made down at the lake." He went to a chest in the corner and rummaged around until he found a large white handkerchief. "There, 'twill be the very thing. Come on!"

So Martha put on her coat and mittens and hood, and she wrapped the white shawl around Lady Flora's shoulders. With the doll tucked in the crook of her arm, she ran down the stairs behind Duncan.

"Found a bit of wood floating in the lake, I did," Duncan said as they puffed down the hill. "I've rigged it up like a skiff. All it wants is a sail."

The day was cold and dull, with heavy clouds hanging low in the sky. The stones at the water's edge were the same dull gray as the clouds, and the water had a flat, hard look to it. Geese called to each other from across the lake.

On the gravel of the shore was a thick piece of wood as long as Martha's arm. Duncan had tied two sticks together in the shape of a cross. He stuck the cross into a crack in the wood, and that was the mast of the boat. Duncan looked very proud as he tied the handkerchief onto the mast. Martha did not think it looked much like a boat, and she said so.

"As if you knew aught about boats!" Duncan cried. "Just you wait until you see it on the water. It ought to have a crew, though. Happen I'll go back for me tin soldiers."

"You ought to try it on the water first," said Martha.

Duncan tied a bit of string to the mast and carefully set the little boat in the water. It bobbed from side to side but did not sink.

"There!" Duncan cried triumphantly. "She's seaworthy, she is." He gave the boat a shove and watched it sail away from the shore. There was not enough wind to fill the sail, but Duncan held tightly to the string anyway. He said she was a beauty, and he'd not let her get away from him.

"But I want to try her with a crew," he said again. "Do us a favor, Martha, and run back up to the house for me soldiers."

He gave her a pleading look, and Martha sighed and said she would go. She set Lady Flora carefully on a large flat stone so that she could watch the boat sail while Martha was gone.

"Mind she doesna fall off and soil her gown!" she called to Duncan as she ran up the hill.

When she hurried into the house, Cook was standing at the bottom of the stairs looking up. She jumped when she saw Martha behind her.

"Och, ye liddle minx! Expecting you to come the other way, I was. Where have you been? I've got the haggis bag all cleaned and ready, and here I've been callin' ye from the nursery these last five minutes."

"Oh!" Martha had forgotten about the haggis. Pulling off her coat and mittens, she followed Cook into the kitchen. Duncan would just have to wait for his soldiers.

The kitchen fire was blazing hot. In a small pot of water over the fire was the stomach of a sheep, which Cook had cleaned well before putting it on to boil. Also in the pot were the sheep's liver, lungs, and heart. They would go into the filling of the haggis, and the stomach-bag would hold it all.

"The pluck ought to be ready," Cook said. With her long spoon she lifted out the lungs and heart and liver. She drained them and put them on her chopping board.

"There now," she said. "Mind yer liddle fingers while I mince these." She chopped everything into tiny bits, and then she asked Martha to bring her the chunk of beef she had ready on the hearth. Cook minced that as well and pushed all the minced meats aside. Then she chopped up a cake of dried animal fat called suet, and some onions.

"Miss Martha, happen ye could grab me

two big handfuls of meal out of the barrel yon," Cook said. Martha ran to the meal barrel and scooped up as much oatmeal as she could fit in her fists. When she got back to the table, Cook had gathered the minced meats and suet and onions into a big heap.

"Just ye sprinkle that meal over this lot as I mix it," Cook said. She kneaded everything together with her hands. Martha stood on tiptoe beside her and let the meal sift out of her hands a little at a time. Cook mixed and mixed, and when all the meal was mixed in, she said it was time to season it. She sprinkled on sage and pepper and mixed it in well with her hands.

"Might I put in the salt?" Martha asked, and Cook said she might.

Then Cook took the stomach out of the boiling water and drained it well. She put it in a bowl of cold water to cool it, and then she took a needle and thread and sewed up the narrow opening at the top of the stomach. She cut a much bigger hole across the widest part, for the meat mixture to go in.

"Would ye rather hauld it or stuff it?" she asked Martha.

"Stuff it," Martha answered promptly. The spiced, minced meats felt strange and squishy in her fingers, but it was fun to scoop the mixture into the stomach-bag. It was like stuffing a feather pillow, only the meat did not fly out of her hands the way feathers did. She thought feathers were nicer to feel but haggis was much nicer to eat.

Cook helped her get the last bits of meat inside the bag, and then Cook poured in a little beef broth. Cook sent Martha to wash her hands while she sewed up the slit. Just before she closed the opening altogether, Cook pressed on the bag to get all the air out. Then she sewed the last bit closed and put the whole thing back into the kettle of water.

"There! It wants two hours' boiling, and a finer haggis ye'll nivver have seen," Cook said, nodding her head in satisfaction. Martha did not see how she could wait until tomorrow to eat it. Cook said happen a seedcake would help, and she took one out of a big jar she had filled yesterday.

"It's a wonder we've no had Duncan in here beggin' seedcakes fifteen times already," Cook said. "Near worrited me to death yesterday when I was bakin' them, him wi' his big eyes all filled wi' that look o' his that nae woman alive can resist."

"Och, Duncan's soldiers!" Martha cried out. "Supposed to bring them down to the lake, I was," she told Cook.

"His own legs was workin', last time I checked," Cook said tartly. She gave Martha a seedcake to take to Duncan. Martha tucked it into her dust-gown pocket before running upstairs to fetch the tin soldiers from the nursery.

She raced back to the lake with the soldiers in hand. Duncan looked up guiltily when he heard her. It took Martha only a second to see why. Lady Flora was not on her stone chair. She was lying on Duncan's boat, staring up at the sky. Her white cap and green skirt stood out bright as flowers against the gray water.

"Duncan!" Martha screamed. "You get her back here!"

"I got tired of waiting," Duncan muttered. "Anyhow, she's all right. That's the sturdiest boat ever set sail."

"I dinna care," Martha snapped. "Pull her back in, now. Or I'll tell Father. Here's your old soldiers." She flung them to the ground at Duncan's feet.

Duncan sighed and began to tug the board back to shore. It had floated a long way out; the string was stretched to its length.

Martha watched anxiously. The boat bobbed from side to side, splashing up little drops of water as it moved.

"Mind her gown!" Martha scolded. "That's her good—"

She choked to a stop in the middle of the sentence. The board had wobbled a bit too far to one side and water rushed up onto its surface.

"She's riding lower from the weight of the doll," Duncan said slowly.

"It's going to sink!" Martha wailed.

"Nay, I'll not let that happen," Duncan said, but he looked worried. "Just give me a minute's peace to gentle her in."

"But Flora's getting all wet!"

The bright green linen was turning dark where water was seeping through. Water licked at the lacy white cap, and the little woolen shawl Martha had knitted turned from snowy white to gray.

Duncan did not say anything now; he only bit his lip and tugged slowly on the string. But it was no use. The woollen shawl soaked up the water and grew very heavy. The boat sank lower and lower in the water.

"She's going to drown!" Martha cried.

"Nay—" Duncan began, tugging harder on the string. The stick mast suddenly slipped to the side and the linen handkerchief slumped half in the water and half over Lady Flora's sodden skirt. Now the boat was heavier on one side, and it slowly tilted up, one edge raising out of the water. Lady Flora began to slide.

Martha opened her mouth to shout but

nothing came out. She watched in horror as her doll slid off the board and into the lake.

"Dinna worry," Duncan said, sounding very worried. "Flora canna sink. She's made of wood."

But the heavy dress and wet shawl weighed down the painted piece of wood that was Martha's doll. The green skirts puffed up, darkened, and were dragged down. Slowly Lady Flora's sweet, familiar face sank beneath the water.

Martha rushed forward, meaning to grab the doll before she sank all the way to the bottom. But Duncan grabbed her arm and pulled her back.

"Martha, nay! You mustn't. You'll catch your death, and anyhow, you ken you canna swim!"

"I care not!" Martha sobbed. "She'll be drowned!"

"She's drowned already, Martha," Duncan whispered. His voice sounded like crying too. "I'm sorry, truly I am."

The linen sail and the mast sticks were

gone. Lady Flora was gone. All that was left was the wet board, floating light as a leaf now that its passenger had sunk to the bottom of Loch Caraid.

Hogmanay

S uddenly it was here, the day Martha had been waiting for, Hogmanay—Old Year's Day. Cook was anxious all morning to see if the sun would shine. Sun on the last day of the year would bring good luck in the year to come.

But Martha didn't care if the sun shone or not. She did not see how her luck could get much worse. Lady Flora was gone. There could never be a doll as beautiful as she had been, and if there was, Martha didn't want it. She hated to put on her petticoat that morning

240

when all she could think of was Lady Flora's wee matching petticoat cold and wet at the bottom of the lake. But Grisie told her she had better dress warmly or she would catch her death and miss all the fun of Hogmanay.

Sunrise was late on winter mornings, and it was nearly nine o'clock before the sky over the Creag began to show a faint pink blush. By then the house was alive with chattering tongues and busy hands. Everyone was in a rush, getting ready for that night's celebration.

By noontime the sun was bright. The sky was white as a cloud, but there were no clouds in it. It was a cold, clear, wintry sky. A sharp wind jounced the branches of the young elms at the edge of the stubbly flax field. Like everyone else, the wind was in a hurry today. It pushed Martha from behind and made her run when she went out to watch Mollie air the linens for the guest room.

"Aisy goes it, lass," Mollie scolded. "Here, hauld out yer arms."

Mollie was brisk and impatient today, thinking of all the things that must be done. She laid the stack of folded sheets on Martha's outstretched arms. Then she took the top sheet off the stack and shook it out vigorously. The sheet flapped in the wind and nearly flew right out of Mollie's grasp, as if it were a big patch of the white sky that wanted to sail back up high where it belonged. Martha would have liked to do the flapping part, and let Mollie stand waiting with the stack of sheets. But Mollie said she was too small to air out the sheets without trailing the ends on the damp ground.

"Indeed," Mollie told her, "yer that small, ye'd likely get carried off by the wind like a schooner w' her sails up!"

Martha did not like to think of boats and sails, for that reminded her of Lady Flora. "No, I wouldna," she said indignantly. "I've got me heavy boots on."

Mollie's laugh rippled above the rippling sheets. "Och, she's her father's daughter, is this one." Her deft hands refolded the sheet and slipped it to the bottom of the stack Martha was holding. One by one she shook out the linens, letting the wind carry off any dust or staleness they might have gathered since the last washing. She folded each one and slid it to the bottom of the stack, until the first sheet she had shaken was back at the top of the pile on Martha's arms.

Then Mollie took the whole stack and turned back toward the house. Martha trailed along behind her, feeling as if the long day would never creep toward evening. Everyone was busy. Mum was packing baskets of presents for Father to take to all the tenant families. She had knitted fourteen pairs of mittens for the children on the estate, and Grisie had knitted seven. After dinner Father took the baskets around to each cottage. Last year he had taken Alasdair along. This year he took Grisie and Robbie too. Martha had begged to go, but Father said briskly that she and Duncan must stay to help Mum and the servants get ready for the party. Uncle Harry and Aunt Grisell and the cousins would be arriving soon, and so would Laird Alroch.

Duncan was the last person Martha wanted

to be left with today. When she saw him beckoning to her from the stable, she turned her back on him and walked furiously toward the house.

"Och, Martha, dinna be cross," he begged. "Please? I told you I was sorry! I'm sorrier than the red cow when it sank in the peat bog. I'll get you a new doll, I promise!"

"I dinna want it!" Martha yelled, without turning around. She was too mad. "Lady Flora was the best doll in the world!"

Her cheeks flamed. She would never forgive him, never. She stalked away from him into the house and wandered out to the kitchen. The kitchen felt stifling hot compared to the cold, sharp wind outside, and it was crowded today. Two of Nannie's sisters had been called in to help with the cooking. In the center of the noise and bustle was Mum, looking flushed and excited. The bannocks for tonight must be baked by Mum's own hands, to bring good luck to all who ate them. It was a whole afternoon's job, for she must make a lot. All the cottagers and half the village would knock on the door of the Stone House that evening, and no one must be sent away empty-handed. It was a Hogmanay tradition.

Cook hovered over Mum all through the baking. Mum could prepare as fine a meal as Cook could, any day, but Cook hated to see her do it. She worried and fussed and predicted dire happenings. The grease would spatter and stain Mum's gown, or burn a hole right through to the skin. Mum laughed and said it was only an old woolen work dress, and she could patch a hole right up. In that case Cook was sure the grease would land on her ladyship's dear hands and raise a fearful blister, and her ladyship would miss all the fun that night.

"As if I'd let a blister spoil my Hogmanay!" Mum retorted. She took out a small bowl and poured into it some melted fat from a pan of sausage that was sizzling on the hearth.

Cook sighed and turned back to the pot of broth she was stirring, glaring at it fiercely as if daring the boiling liquid to spatter so much as one droplet in Mum's direction.

"There you are!" Mum said to Martha. "I wondered where you'd got to. How's my lass this afternoon? Did you make it up with Duncan?"

Martha shrugged her shoulders. Mum gave her a long look.

"It's not well to carry a quarrel into the new year," she said gently. "Duncan has been punished, and it's truly sorry he is that your bonny doll is lost."

Still Martha said nothing. She climbed onto a stool to watch Mum make the bannocks. She liked to watch Mum's hands fly as she kneaded ground oats and melted fat into a paste. She liked the way the round cakes of dough sizzled when Mum fried them in the big iron pan over the fire. Mum gave her a cake, fresh from the pan and stinging hot.

Martha couldn't help but grow excited as evening approached. There was a hollow space in her stomach that seemed to choke with tears every time she thought of Lady Flora. How bonny she had looked in her fine holiday gown! But the oatcake had filled up a tiny corner of the hollow space, and then the house began to fill up with guests and it was so noisy that Martha could not hear the quiet space inside her.

Uncle Harry arrived first, with his big family. Their carriage rolled into the courtyard just as Father appeared at the top of the hill. Grisie and Alisdair were just behind him, their faces red from the wind. Grisie ran to greet the cousins as they climbed out of the carriage. She always liked to see Janet and Meg, Uncle Harry's oldest daughters. Mary and Rachel were Martha's age, and there were David and Harold in between, and baby Eamonn in Aunt Grisell's arms.

It was already growing dark, and the wind was far too bitter for standing outside. Everyone hurried into the parlor. Mum was waiting by the pianoforte in her beautiful red gown with its great bell-shaped skirt. There was a loud confusion of coats and shawls being taken off, and peats being heaped on the fire, and Uncle Harry thwacking Father and Alisdair and Robbie on the back, and a great roar of laughter when he thwacked Mum by mistake.

"She's getting soft, is my sister!" Uncle Harry boomed. "I remember a time when she'd have walloped me right back!"

"I'd wallop you still," Mum laughed, "but I fear I'd lay you flat! 'Twould be a pity to have you snoring all through our Hogmanay."

Martha loved to listen to Mum and Uncle Harry tease each other. Mum's cheeks flushed red and she looked nearly as young as Grisie, laughing up at her big, curly-haired brother. Uncle Harry was so loud and jolly that sometimes you forgot Aunt Grisell was in the room. She was thin and pale and quiet, with gentle eyes. Martha liked her very much, but she liked Uncle Harry best.

Then Robbie looked out the window and shouted that another carriage was coming. Laird Alroch had arrived. Sandy went out to help the old laird's driver put away the horses and the carriage. Father's carriage had been moved into the cow-house, for there was not enough room in the carriage house for three coaches.

While Father and Uncle Harry greeted Laird Alroch with a toast of whiskey, Martha slipped into the kitchen to watch the bustle of preparations. Mollie squeezed past her in the doorway, holding high a platter of sliced roast beef in one hand and a tureen of soup in the other.

"Look sharp, Miss Martha," she said cheerily. "Ye dinna want a crock o' broth comin' doon upon ye to muss yer pretty frock!"

The kitchen was a blur of bodies rushing to and fro. The table was filled with dishes of food, some of them waiting to be carried out to the parlor and others to be eaten by the servants when things calmed down a bit. Cook and Mollie and the others would have their own holiday feast in the kitchen during the family's meal.

Uncle Harry's coachman and Laird Alroch's coachman were warming their hands at the fire. Cook gave them each a cup of ale, warning them to stay out of the way of those whose work was not yet finished. She had changed into her best clothes, and she was an imposing sight in her black wool dress and her best

white apron, so stiffly starched that it crackled when she moved. Her face was redder than
ever, and her eyes looked every direction at
once. But Martha could see that she was enjoy-
ing herself immensely. Cook loved to have
extra people to order around.

Nannie, bright and fresh in her own Sunday
frock, smiled at Martha from the kitchen
table and beckoned her over for a taste of
the almond-cream she was whipping. Eagerly
Martha ran to lick the spoon. She closed her
eyes and let the sweet, nut-flavored cream
melt on her tongue.

"'Tis like a spoonful of cloud," she said to
Nannie.

Nannie laughed and said, "Ye'd best flit
back to the parlor before Cook puts ye to
work, miss!"

"I heard that, Nan Jenkins." Cook's voice
boomed over Martha's head. But when Martha
turned to look at her, Cook was smiling broadly.
She put a hand under Martha's chin. "Och,
look at the bonny wee thing in her fine feathers," she said tenderly, admiring Martha's dress.

"That green is just the shade to bring oot the fire in yer hair. Noo—off ye go back to the parlor. Mollie's got the table near about ready, and yer mither will be sittin' doon any minute."

She turned back to the hearth. With a last wistful glance at the bowl of almond-cream, Martha ran out of the kitchen and back into the parlor. Everything was ready now for the feast. Tall candles flamed above the silver candlesticks in the center of the long parlor table. There was so much food on the table that she could hardly see the embroidered tablecloth. There was pigeon pie and boiled lamb, boiled chicken and sheep's-head broth. There were two puddings and three kinds of jelly, and bread and potatoes and a round of venison. There was the rich, tasty haggis. It was Father's favorite, and Martha's too. The sideboard groaned beneath its load of desserts.

Father stood at the table and cleared his throat. It was time for him to say grace. Everyone was quiet. He began the long prayer that thanked God for the bountiful feast and the good health of the family. Martha closed her eyes tight so she would not be tempted to peek at the platters of delicious food. She was afraid her stomach would growl loud enough for everyone to hear over Father's prayer.

At last grace was over, and it was time to eat. Nearly every chair was filled at the long table. Uncle Harry joked that he couldn't tell which plate was his to eat off. Mum said he was just using that as an excuse to eat off the three plates nearest him, and the people sitting next to him had better look sharp or he'd make off with their beef.

Martha, giggling, caught Duncan's eye. He grinned at her eagerly. Once, a long time ago, they had promised each other to always be good friends like Mum and Uncle Harry. But Uncle Harry had never drowned Mum's doll. Martha scowled at Duncan and looked away. She laughed and whispered with cousin Mary. She took slow, tiny bites of her haggis, to make the delicious taste last longer. She looked everywhere and smiled at everyone but Duncan. She filled the hollow space in her stomach with almond-cream and sweetmeats.

Somehow, though, the hollow space seemed to be growing larger. Martha ate until she had eaten too much, and her stomach felt uncomfortably full. But right on top of that was the aching empty spot. She wanted Lady Flora. She wanted everything to be like it had been yesterday, when Lady Flora was in her arms and there was all the excitement of Hogmanay to look forward to. Now that Hogmanay was here, Martha felt cheated. She should be having more fun. All her kin were guffawing between bites and laughing with their eyes when their mouths were full.

Except Duncan. His eyes were sad. Martha felt angrier when she saw that. She felt as though she were spoiling his holiday, when really it was the other way around. She wished he were not sitting across from her so that she wouldn't have to look at him.

Then supper was over, and Mollie and Nannie came to collect the empty dishes. The table was moved against a wall. Mum sat down at the pianoforte. Everyone clustered around her. She began to sing:

*"I had a wee hen, and I loved it well,
I fed my hen on yonder hill."*

Everyone joined in.

*"My hen, chuckie-chuckie, chuckie-chuckie,
coo,
Everyone loves their hen, why should I not
love my hen too?"*

This was the best part of Hogmanay, the singing—and the presents. Everyone had a present on Hogmanay night. There was even a little package for Tullie Grayshanks. Cook had made the brownie a new shirt and trousers, and a little gray jacket. She said she would leave the package for Tullie with his bread and cream that night.

"We canna have him thinkin' he's no a part o' the family!" Cook told Martha when she brought in the wee bundle.

"I wish I could see him," Martha said.

"He's that skittish, I doubt ye ivver will, lass," Cook told her. "Ye must just be glad in yer heart that he's here." She smiled. "Ah—here's yer mither wi' the rest o' the gifts!"

Mum came into the parlor with a big rush basket. It was filled with mysterious rag bundles. Each bundle was tied around with a ribbon, and the ends of the ribbons trailed out of the basket. There was a name embroidered on each trailing end.

Mum placed the basket in the middle of the room, and there was a mad scramble as each child raced to find the ribbon with his or her name on it. Martha ducked under elbows until she found the fluttering bit of silk with her name on it. It was a dark green ribbon that just matched her dress, and she could use it for her hair later. Martha tugged on the ribbon, trying to follow it to the bundle at its other end. There was a riot of laughter and friendly scuffling as ribbons tangled and cousins collided. Uncle Harry's hearty laugh rang out above the noise.

Martha's bundle was long and skinny. She tore off the scrap of cloth. Inside was a pair of knitting needles. They were made of wood, and they were smooth and straight. She had never seen such lovely needles. Their pointed ends were not too sharp, and their other ends were round and flat, so that the loops of yarn would not slip off when she was knitting. They were just the right size for Martha's hands.

"Oh, Mum!" she said. Mum smiled at her.

"Thank your father, my dear," she said. "He had the choosing of them, when he went to Perth."

Martha gave Father a kiss on the cheek. He pretended to be gruff, but she could see that he was pleased she liked his gift so well. Duncan gave a shout of joy and came running to thank Father for the new set of paints. Martha brushed past him and ran to show her needles to Rachel and Mary. Then the hollow place inside throbbed a little when she remembered that she could not knit any more wee clothes for Lady Flora. The thought made her scowl.

"Such a grim face for such a bonny lass," Laird Alroch said, ruffling her hair. His kind eyes twinkled down at her.

Martha remembered the present she had made him. She ran to the sideboard and grabbed the soft package. Feeling shy, she held it out to Laird Alroch.

"What's all this, then?" said the old laird. He unwrapped the package and took the two gloves into his hands. There was a look of wonder on his face.

"Spun the wool and knit them meself, I did," Martha said.

Laird Alroch's eyes glistened. "The dear wee lass," he said. He put a hand on Martha's cheek. Suddenly she threw her arms around his neck and hugged, hard. She thought it must feel the same way to hug your grandfather, if you had one.

Now there was more singing, and soon came a knock at the door.

"Quick, the bannocks!" Mum cried. Someone pushed a basket into her hands and she moved swiftly to open the door.

"Hurrah!" cried the crowd of boys standing in the chill night air. Their noses and cheeks were pink, and their breath made frosty clouds around their faces. They sang in rough, cheery voices:

> *"Get up, gude wife, and binna sweer,*
> *An' deal yer bread to them that's here,*
> *For the time'll come whan ye'll be dead,*
> *An' then ye'll need neither ale nor bread."*

Martha crowded close to watch. She thought it would be fun to join them, to go singing at the doors of every house on the estate. They started at Father's house, because Father was the laird. She felt proud of Father. But she wished he would let her go to sing for oatcakes with the other children. Her brothers and the boy cousins were putting on their caps. They could go, because they were boys. Even Duncan was allowed to go. It did not seem fair that she and Grisie must stay home, when even the farmers' daughters went singing too.

Mum handed the basket around. Each boy took one oatcake and then Mum said they might each take another. There were so many baskets of cakes still in the kitchen. Martha slipped her hand in and took an oatcake as the basket went past, and Mum pretended not to notice.

It was very late now, but Martha was not at all tired. She wanted to stay awake till midnight, to see who would be first foot. The first person to set foot in the house after midnight would have extra good luck in the new year. There was a lot of joking and guessing about who it would be this year. Uncle Harry said it was sure to be his son, David, and Father was certain it would be Robbie. It could not be Alisdair, because of his red hair. It would bring very bad luck upon the whole household if the first foot was a redhead. No one could explain to Martha why that was so. That meant she could never be first foot herself, even if she were a boy and could go out singing with the others.

But it did not matter much. Tonight it was just as nice to be home where everyone was singing and dancing and telling stories. Grisie played the pianoforte, and then Mum made Martha play a little tune. Laird Alroch clapped and clapped and said he'd nivver heard such fine playing in all his days.

Uncle Harry sang a song about Finn MacChumhail and the lady giant who taught him to forge iron. Aunt Grisell told the story of the time Bonnie Prince Charlie had spent the night in her brother's room, long ago when she was a little girl living far away in the north. Martha asked Mum to tell the story of the water fairy and the stone man, but Mum said she would never get through it—she was all the time jumping up to answer the door and hand oatcakes round to the singing visitors. Mollie and Nannie begged Mum to let them do the door-opening and oatcake-passing, but Mum said she wouldna hear of it, she was having as much fun as the bairns.

Laird Alroch began a tale. His wavery voice flickered up and down like the fire. Martha felt herself staring very hard at the fire, and then her head was resting on Grisie's lap and Grisie was stroking her hair. She was sure she was still wide awake. But things seemed to swirl around before her eyes and all the stories got mixed up together. The lady giant was telling Prince Charlie not to worry, Lady Flora was not turned to stone. She had only gone to live in Loch Caraid with the water fairy. The water fairy would not be lonely now that she had a bonny doll to love.

Suddenly everyone was standing and Father was taking out the green glass bottle of claret wine, and Martha knew that it was midnight already. She could not remember the end of Laird Alroch's story. But if she closed her eyes she could see the water fairy combing the long floating strands of Lady Flora's hair with a willow twig. She wanted to see the water fairy more than ever now, to know if she really was taking care of Flora.

Father poured a glass of claret for each of the adults. It was toasting time. For the first time all day, except during Father's prayer before the meal, the room grew quiet. Father held up his glass.

"May the good Lord hold us all in His hand, this year and always," he said in his low, solemn voice.

"Aye," said Uncle Harry, raising his glass.

"Finer words nivver were spoken," said Laird Alroch. Everyone took a drink. Martha pretended her tea was claret, but she didn't know what claret tasted like. She thought it must be sour, because Grisie pursed her lips in a funny way after she took a sip. This was the first year Grisie was allowed a glass of the wine. Martha sipped her tea and pursed up her lips, practicing for claret.

Now it was Mum's turn. She lifted her glass and made her toast.

"May our hearts be filled with love, our minds with wisdom, and our bodies with health."

"Och, me lass," said Laird Alroch, "finer words nivver were spoken."

Uncle Harry said in his booming voice, "May the wind of sorrow ne'er blow open our door."

"Finer words nivver were spoken, me boy," croaked Laird Alroch. Cousin Mary gave Martha a nudge. Every year, Laird Alroch said the same thing about every single toast. Martha choked back a giggle. It would not do to laugh at such a solemn moment.

Grisie spoke up shyly. "May our fires burn bright and our water run clear." Her voice could hardly be heard. Martha could not wait till she was old enough to make a toast. She would make certain that everyone heard her.

The toasts went around the room, each one punctuated by Laird Alroch's praise and the sound of glasses being drunk from and sometimes refilled. Grisie's glass was still quite full. Her mouth, Martha could see, was more pursed than ever.

When it came Laird Alroch's turn, he gave Mum a long, beaming look before speaking.

"May blessings rain down upon this fine lady, as she pours them oot on those around her," he said. Mum's eyes grew suddenly glistening.

"Finer words were never spoken, sir," said Father seriously. He looked into Mum's eyes and drained his glass. For a moment the hollow space in Martha's middle rose to her throat in a great happy lump. Father was like a mirror of Mum's own face, reflecting back a great light of love. Martha felt warmed all over by it. She was glad to be her particular self in this particular family. There could be no nicer family in all the world than Father and Mum, and Grisie and Alisdair and Robbie and—Duncan.

The happy lump dropped back into her middle and became a cold hollow space again.

Just then came another loud knock at the door. Everyone jumped and laughed. The first foot had come. There was a hush in the air while everyone waited to see who it would be.

"Great lairds of thunder!" cried Uncle Harry.

The door had opened upon Duncan. He was panting as if he had run very hard. Around the rim of his cap his dark hair was studded with droplets of water, for a light, cold rain had begun to fall.

He stepped inside and held out a bottle and a little cloth sack. It was another Hogmanay custom that the person who set first foot inside the house must bring certain gifts: whiskey, bread, a little salt.

After the first surprised silence there was a roar of greeting. Father gave Duncan a little clap on the back.

"You've made clever work, my lad, to beat out your brothers," he said.

"And my David!" roared Uncle Harry approvingly. Uncle Harry always appreciated a good joke.

"Where be they?" Father asked. "Still carousing in the cottages?"

"I canna say, Father," Duncan said. He was still out of breath. "I—I didna go with them. I had—an errand to run."

"What's this?" Father asked, drawing his brows together in the beginnings of his stern look.

"Peace, Allan," Mum said lightly. "Shall we stand here shivering wi' the door wide open?" She spoke the traditional words. "Enter, Duncan Morse, and be welcome."

She ushered him inside and hurried him to the fire. His ears and nose were red as Mum's gown. When he spoke, his words tumbled over each other. He said that he had gone to Auld Mary's cottage. Father and Mum were surprised. It was a long walk in the daytime, and now it was a bitter cold and rainy night.

"You must be frozen through, lad!" Mum exclaimed.

"Auld Mary gave me some soup," Duncan said. "She had it waiting for me. Said she was expecting me, she did!"

Mum and Father exchanged a look. A chill went down Martha's spine. Had Auld Mary really known Duncan was coming? Perhaps she did have the second sight after all.

"But why ever did you go there, boy?" Father said sternly. "Miles across the moor, alone, at night!"

Duncan looked nervous but resolute. "I had to, sir," he said. "Wanted to make it up to Martha, I did, for losing her doll on the loch. You ken Auld Mary makes dolls. I thought she could trade me one for my new paint set."

Martha's mouth dropped open. She heard Mum gasp. Duncan had gone all the way across the moor to sell his brand-new paints! He had wanted those paints for months.

"But she didn't have any," he went on, "at least not the kind I was thinking of. But she gave me this." He turned to Martha and thrust a bundle into her arms.

"It's nothing like your fine Lady Flora, Martha," he said. "I don't ken as you'll care for it at all. But Auld Mary said you'd like it."

Martha stared at the bundle. She felt dazed. It was a scrap of coarse handspun flannel wrapped around something hard. Duncan watched her with anxious eyes.

Slowly she unwrapped the bundle. It was a small, plain wooden box. The top of the box lifted off. Inside were a tiny wooden table and two tiny chairs. The backs of the chairs and the legs of the table were carved with the most delicate little vines and dainty flowers. The chair seats were woven from oat-straw. There was a cauldron made of a hollowed-out acorn. There was a wee cradle with rockers on the bottom. It rocked on Martha's palm when she picked it up. Inside the cradle was the tiniest of babies, with a muslin head and a little soft body all wrapped in silk.

Best of all were the mother and father dolls. They too were made of muslin, and their eyes

and mouths were bits of bright thread. The mother doll wore a dress of gauzy blue, with a cunning little hat that looked exactly like a bluebell. The father doll had brown knee-breeches and a green blouse, and his cap was apple red. Both dolls had pointed muslin ears.

"Oh, Duncan," Martha breathed. She had never seen anything so lovely in her life.

"Auld Mary says it belonged to a fairy's bairn," said Duncan. "She found it on the moor the night after the fairies' last dance. She says the Wee Folk won't take back a toy after it's been lost, and so she brought it home, and then a cock crowed three times and so she kenned it was meant for you. I dinna ken how," he finished, "but she said it was so, true as I breathe."

"Your paints," Martha said in a tiny voice.

"Auld Mary wouldna take them," said Duncan. "She said she'd not trade for what she'd only found, and what was meant for someone else in the first place. But I'm to paint a picture for her, she says."

"What about the whiskey and the salt?"

Father asked. He did not like to take things without paying for them.

"She made me take them, Father," said Duncan. "She said it would bring good luck on her for the giving."

Father nodded, accepting. "We must all go over tomorrow to thank her," said Mum.

Before anyone else could speak, there came a pounding at the door. It was Alisdair, Robbie, and David, all out of breath and the two with dark hair jostling to be in front. Uncle Harry burst into his great roaring laugh, and that set everyone else laughing. The three boys laughed the loudest when they understood the joke. None of them could be first foot, for Duncan had beaten them to it.

The hollow space in Martha's middle was filling up. It was filling with Uncle Harry's booming laughter, and Mum's light high laugh like the rippling of a brook, and the proud smiling glow in Father's eyes. It was filling with the good luck of the New Year, the miles of windy moor between the Stone House and Auld Mary's rough cottage, the noise and teasing of

270

her brothers and sister and cousins. It was filling with Duncan's happy grin. It was full— it was gone. There was no hollow space inside. There was only a good sort of ache that made her want to hug Duncan.

"You're a grand brother." She whispered it, but everyone heard. "I'm glad I'm your sister."

"Finer words, lass," said old Laird Alroch, "nivver were spoken."

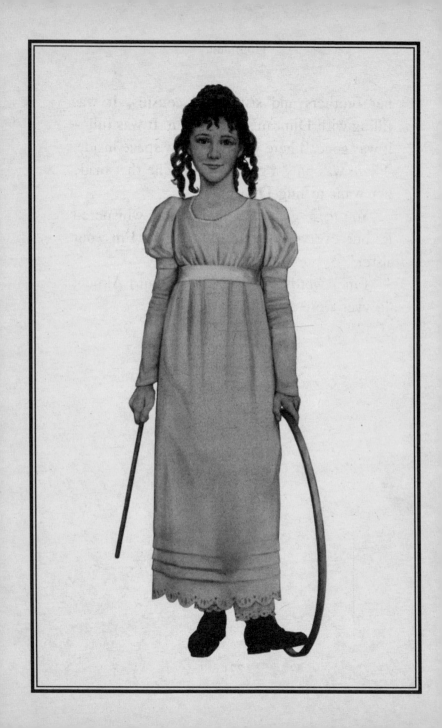

Introducing
Charlotte!

Laura Ingalls Wilder wrote the Little House books about her childhood growing up on the prairies and frontiers of America. Laura's grandmother was Charlotte Tucker, and now you can read about *her* childhood in a brand-new series of Little House books.

Travel back in time to 1814 and meet Charlotte when she was a little girl. Charlotte lives in the town of Roxbury, near the bustling city of Boston. Life in the Tuckers' house is pleasant and merry, but Charlotte's family worries about the war that's been going on since 1812. What will the year ahead bring for Charlotte and the Tucker family?

You can read about Charlotte's childhood days in *Little House by Boston Bay*. Like the Little House books about Laura Ingalls, Rose Wilder, Caroline Quiner, and Martha Morse, *Little House by Boston Bay* is a glimpse into the past, as seen through the eyes of another young girl from America's beloved Little House family.

Little House by Boston Bay is the first in an ongoing series of novels about the adventures of Charlotte Tucker.

Come Home to
Little House

The LAURA *Years*
By Laura Ingalls Wilder
Illustrated by Garth Williams

The ROSE *Years*

By Roger Lea MacBride
Illustrated by Dan Andreasen
& David Gilleece

The CAROLINE *Years*

By Maria D. Wilkes
Illustrated by Dan Andreasen

Other LITTLE HOUSE *titles you may enjoy:*

Ask for these titles at your favorite bookstore!